Praise for Richard Thieme

"Your mind is a door I didn't know existed."

"The depth, complexity and texture of Thieme's thought processes break the mold." — Brian Snow, Senior Technical Director, NSA (ret.)

"I quite liked your story. I've been reading science fiction lately and yours was right up there." — John Updike, author

"Give me Richard Thieme. His mind is in orbit but his feet are on the ground." — Dan Geer, CISO, In-Q-Tel (CIA)

"I am deeply grateful to you... one seldom finds one so sympathetic and discerning. Once on a snowy morning in Moscow, Boris Spassky declaimed four pages of Bullet Park in Russian. I was very encouraged as I am by you." — John Cheever, author

"Thieme's very imaginative writing has a complexity that raises the narrative to the fringes of slipstream. We're left wondering what's real and what's not." — Steven Pirie, *The Future Fire*, UK

"Thieme takes us to the edges of cliffs we know are there but rarely visit. He wonderfully weaves together life, mystery, and passion with creativity and imagination." — Clinton C. Brooks, Senior Adviser for Homeland Security and Asst. Deputy Director, NSA (ret.)

Richard Thieme earned his 'wings' in cyberspace. He shares his intelligence - his brilliance, really - as he steers his starship through the stars." — Jennifer Leigh Marais, science writer in South Africa.

"Beautiful descriptions and intriguing concepts" — *The Fix* (UK)

"Thieme is truly an oracle for the Matrix generation." — Kim Zetter, author of *Countdown to Zero Day*.

"Richard Thieme: *Genius!*" — Thuthuka Sithole, a Zulu security researcher in South Africa

"Richard Thieme sees deeply into the nature of the human spirit and expresses with great clarity what he observes." — Joel Garreau, *Washington Post*

"You are a practitioner of *wu wei*, the effort to choose the elegant appropriate contribution to each and every issue you address." — Hal McConnell, NSA analyst (ret.)

"Richard Thieme's clarity of thinking is refreshing and his insights are profound." — Bruce Schneier, author and security guru

"Richard Thieme teaches experts to see with 'beginners' eyes and hackers to think like philosophers. More than a great thinker, Thieme is an original soul. When you read Richard Thieme, you believe in *The Matrix*." — Sol Tzvi, Senior Security Practitioner, formerly with Microsoft Israel, rock star, and entrepreneur

"Richard Thieme has inspired me to see myself and the world around me in a different light. His writing represents a glimpse into the inner workings of a most extraordinary mind." — Becky Bace. NSA (ret.)

"Thieme's writing illuminates unorthodox but deeply profound ways of understanding ourselves and everything around us." — Jennifer Granick, Director of Civil Liberties at the Stanford University Center for Internet and Society

"Thieme's words more than inspire, they teach us how to think. The reader is left reeling, dizzy with insight." — Robin Roberts, CIA R&D (ret.)

"Richard Thieme is the real Enoch Root." — Anonymous

FOAM

Volume One: Lobes and Folds

Richard Thieme

Exurban Press

Cover illustration by Duncan Long.

Published by Exurban Press.

ISBN 978-0692475515

For Shirley

"The only way you can tell the truth is through fiction." — Clinton Brooks, former Senior Adviser for Homeland Security and Assistant Deputy Director, NSA, to Richard Thieme, in conversation

"In space I had an epiphany, an experience of the connectedness of everything. I later came to understand it. It's where you experience, see the separateness of things with your physical eyes but experience the connectedness of all things in an altered state. From that point on, life was never the same for me. I had to find what these deep issues are, recognizing that our scientific cosmology was incomplete and out religious cosmologies archaic. I was looking for a new myth about ourselves, but by myth I mean truth." — Astronaut Edgar Mitchell, Apollo 14, in conversation with Richard Thieme

"We want you to believe in us, but not too much." — An alien, in conversation with Herbert Schirmer, according to Herbert Schirmer

"The origami UFO model simulates a flying UFO with four anti-gravity generators. If you are a novice in origami, it might be difficult for you to fold. In that case, you need to tackle an easier model and become comfortable with folding techniques, such as the inside-reverse fold which reverses the face of the corner flap to show the inside of the flap. It is essential to know how to apply this folding technique." — http://www.origami-make.com

Table of Contents

Volume One: Lobes and Folds

CHAPTER 1

The Guy in the Flappy Hat

"**I** like that hat!" Heidi said to the guy in the yellow-and-black plaid coat and the brown leather hat with flappy ears. He took it off and grinned, looked at the hat in his cold hands, tilting it into the streetlight so she could see its more subtle features, then replaced it, pulling it tight. Exposed to the wind, the edges of his ears reddened, and the wind brought tears to his eyes. He said loudly, "Mother-*fuck! Damn* this cold!"- a normal remark for a Midwest native but a phrase he had to learn from cable, along with hundreds of others as well as body language, gestures, facial expressions, rehearsing in front of a mirror night after night in cheap motels. *Don't pay more than sixty bucks,* they instructed, or so he thought, trying to distinguish the signal from the noise. *Say what? How much?* He tilted his head, seeking an optimal angle for receiving communications in the elastic space-time of the planet which distorted almost everything, on top of which the tangled thoughts of passengers and the roar of the bus at highway speed (he was sitting near the engine, too, so there was that then on top of it) made it hard to hear. He chose to think he got it right, more or less, and nodded to no one there, not even the seat, and said aloud, "OK, then, the limit is sixty bucks. I got it."

The man beside him looked at him when he spoke, then looked away. Teufel ignored the feelings bleeding from the passenger. He came to earth resembling an automaton, autonomous, defenses at the ready, in that way too like so many humans over twelve.

They must want him to learn to be thrifty and fit in the culture toward which he was riding, zigging and zagging up and down the middle of the country. *Don't call attention to yourself.* That was one of the first rubrics Jack learned, hearing it from Oscar, a detective in a video, thinking it must be meant for him. He heard it again from a woman in line at the coffee shop — days later, after he arrived — which reinforced the rule. He didn't know her name, nor want to know it, really, the older lady good for killing time in line, waiting for orders to be filled, but not appealing carnally, what with her wrinkles, sagging this and that, and obvious (he inferred) dryness. She responded with zest and empathy when he told her he was new in town and asked in a supplicating way, so how can a guy from far away (she had no clue what he meant by that) adapt to this challenging culture?

"Well, it is an odd one," she said, "not exotic, but... they don't know it's a culture. Fish to water, you know. They believe what they see and think what they see is what's there."

"Got it!" Jack grinned and took out his notepad and wrote it down as the woman continued to talk. She recalled her first luncheon at a club.

"That's where I learned the Prime Directive," she said, "just looking around at what people were doing. Keep your purse open, your mouth shut, and wear beige. That pretty much sums it up."

He wrote that down too, not understanding what it meant, but thinking it must be important.

The woman laughed. "That's my advice to you, young man,. Look around, notice what they do, then do it. Don't call attention to yourself."

The line was barely moving and she seemed to want to talk. She came from far away, too, she repeated, and had lived in other countries. You learn to pick up cues and clues to what to do that way. When she arrived, she was "the other woman" as well, going on to relate the story of her first husband, how they grew apart, and then TMI about the one who brought her here, her second and final spouse, she hoped (she said with a laugh). He came for a promotion and she tagged along "to start over." That's the American Way, isn't it? When it hurts too much to stay, we move, and rewrite our history. The editing never ends.

"You follow breadcrumbs through the forest?" Jack said. "Before the birds of time can dine?"

She ignored his vague statement. "Just remember that rule," she said. "In this city, maybe in the upper Midwest as a whole, you don't get a second chance. You wouldn't know Norm Mandel (she said man-DELL) at First Third Bank, would you by any chance?"

Jack shook his head. "The only bank I know is Ehrlichmann and Jewell. They brokered my rented loft."

"E & J. Yes, I know them very well. Anyway, poor Norm came here from Hawaii and didn't have any long sleeve shirts. They invited him to dinner at the Club, because he needed to meet the right people, and his new blue suit was fine but he wore a white short sleeve shirt. His cuffs didn't show. There was nothing but skin at the wrist. You would have thought he showed up naked. Well, that was the end of that. Do you think I'm exaggerating? I'm not. They wrote him off at once. I mean, they wrote him off for-*ever*," her eyes narrowing to show that she meant, indeed, "*forever*." "The poor schmuck. Nothing has worked for the guy, but he has no clue But that's the reason, honestly." She smiled, a co-conspirator of sorts, outsiders looking in. "You need to understand how it works. Even then, you don't stand a chance."

Teufel tried to integrate the meaning of her words with what he learned on the bus. That didn't work. She leaned in and looked at him closely to see what was happening inside, using his eyes as a window as humans do, but nothing was going on in there, not that she could see. "You're not a Jew, by any chance, are you? That would make it worse."

Jack shook his head.

"I am beyond Jew or Christian or Mormon or Moslem or Buddhist or Hindu and on and on. I am not even Unitarian. We outgrew that sort of thing long ago. I am sure it is still useful here."

She tilted her head and looked at him intently. Jack thought of Larry David, doing the scan.

"Where did you say you were from?"

Teufel grinned. "I will tell you the simple truth because you have disclosed so much. You would say, 'another planet,' although to say it that way, to call it a planet, would be as if you said, 'I come from one street north of the expressway near Wolf Cove.' To us, that makes no sense. That way of framing identity disappeared longer ago than you can count. We included and transcended, one might say, everything that came before, every time we flipped. Every meet-up leads to a flip. A flip is a way to say, we become someone/something new, and we choose a new name. Your identities are so entwined with all those religions! That's why, when we say what is real, you get depressed. To understand would mean letting go of who you think you are. Your religions bind your tribes like music. It is effective at a primitive level although also the cause of much horror. Is the trade-off worth it, do you think?" He shrugged. "The evidence is not in yet. You sing hymns and kill one another with gusto, all because of religion. It works for some but obviously not for everyone. But the dead have no vote, the slaughtered have no voice."

"I see," she said, although she could not, having no point of reference. "In any case," she continued, "remember that this is a peasant culture. Difference and Otherness are primary threats. They don't need friends, they have the ones they need from growing up and never moving far. That comforts them —"

"Like the Wasatch Front," Teufel nodded, "which is where in fact I come from, I was just joking, all that about the planets, I am really from Utah. They say the mountains surround them like a mother's embrace, but its the culture, really, that they can't live without."

"It's like that here too," his friend-of-the-moment said. "They may go away for a few years, but just like Mormons after a mission, they scurry back to live inside a shared narrative. That makes them feel safe." She moved up as the one ahead took change and a cappuccino, sipped foam from the edge of the cup, then went to the condiment counter. "The bottom line, young man, is, wear long sleeves and a white shirt. It's a man's version of 'wear beige.'"

She smiled and looked him up and down as if seeing for the first time what he was wearing, his plaid jacket, his flappy hat. "On the other hand," she said, "I don't think it will matter if you

5

wear long sleeves or not."

"I am already one of the damned? Like Fort said of UFOs and rains of toads?"

Before she could answer, she was asked what she wanted. She ordered a pumpkin spice latte with thick foam, extra hot, which Dade the barista used as an occasion to remind the entire line, projecting his voice toward the cold sunlight streaming through the window half way across the shop, "we sell pumpkin spice only until New Year's Day. Peppermint too, our special delicious Christmas latte, ends then too. Get them while you can!" (Dade was the main man, barista for the morning rush, and spent his days behind the wooden counter, his mini-fro inside a red bandanna, the tat on his arm barely discernible because it was dark blue on black.)

Jack took notes on a pad using pen and paper, choosing to act like an old school, twentieth century kind of guy. "Don't call attention." These people were like mirrors, he thought, reflecting one another to calibrate behaviors to some norm, keep each other in the picture, keep the picture in the frame.

He thought again of Oscar and remembered when Racine smashed the glass and took the Circe on the floor. He watched the video on his I-pad in the Timbercreek Inn in Nebraska, shifting on a sagging bed, moving a lot to ease the ache in his arms from holding the pad straight. The CRT in the room could not take a cable, and he had to keep moving to save the connection and keep the movie streaming. "It tends to call attention," Oscar said, trying to help his friend. Jack hit pause and wrote it down. Then he wrote it down again in line, that cold sunny morning, several days later.

Oscar went on, "You're up there banging the widow..." and

Jack grinned at the memory — the widow being banged, not shifting on the old mattress, and he loved how she said, *"You're sore?"* and reached for more ice. He remembered how she looked against the wall before he smashed the glass and fucked her on the floor. Oh, she was so wet, you could feel it despite the lack of tactility or drip, and somehow she avoided being cut by shards. The scene made him sit up and quack like a duck and say to himself, whoa! Daddy! as his hand moved onto himself as if it had a mind of its own, which in a way it did, linked somehow to his dick which did seem have a mind of its own. That was one thing about being human that he liked right away.

He remembered how her fingers dug into the sheets, clawing with concupiscence. She was so supple and her body was so... perfect..."you're so... perfect," Sebastian said, Jack trying to link the two, wondering if she had been made as well — although she later grew as big as the blueberry girl in *Willy Wonka* and didn't appeal anymore. He preferred her young, with her fingers digging into the sheets (satin ones like Jackie O's, which if they weren't changed every time she took a nap, provoked a tantrum from the lispy princess, who raged at her maid in a way that was quite unlike how the press played up her sibilant whisper as a mark of aristocracy rather than affectation — Jack read all about her in *People, Woman, Who* and *Us.*) Meanwhile the lawyer thrust from behind, suggested rather than shown, Jack paying close attention to what he was doing and thinking, he must do that too, once he found a woman he could follow like a hound, once he got a whiff of it. Following the script.

He reviewed those scenes again and again on the bus, rocking through Iowa, the icy window ablaze with sunlight. Jack grinned until the guy beside him, noting the peculiar nature of his grin, looked away with discomfort, wondering what the hell. Jack wasn't wearing ear buds and wasn't lost in song so his animated face made no sense, it syncopated to nothing another human being could see.

Banging a woman will come, Teufel hoped, riding the bus like the Flying Dutchman, feeling as if his trip would never end. And as if a fulfillment of his wishes, when the trip did end at last, three days later, counting days as they did as one light-and-dark turn around the yellow dwarf they called "the sun," here he was in the city, walking on the cold pavement surrounded by holiday crowds with a woman named Heidi who he met that day and wanted to bang soon, like, if not now, when? And if not him, who? as a sage said in a footnote in a book left in some motel. Not the Book of Mormon, there were fewer and fewer of those as he went east and avoided Marriotts. Besides, why else would she be with him, if she didn't want to hook up, a fact he learned from soaps and serials and sitcoms and reality shows like *Naked Dating* (his favorite was *The Bachelor*, although he liked *Gray's* too because of all the gay sex)? Why else would she be with him in the cold, sharing her portable warmth like a potbellied stove, letting him feel her warm presence, brushing his arm with hers, an implicit invitation as the night fell, as the twilight gathered around them like a shawl and lights of the cityscape brightened, why would she be there if she wasn't thinking of a tryst, too, seeing in her mind's eye as he saw in his a tangle of naked limbs dissolving into a fade as the door to the fantasy suite closed, or if on HBO, the door remained open on a plucky couple fucking from all angles, good views all around, panning down their flanks to their loins and the rollicking frolicking sounds of buck buck buck, then afterward, after the woman douched, the guy beating off on the bed like the ugly one on

Girls?

Sixty bucks, he said to himself, was not much. When he plugged "US$60" into web sites looking for a room, most options vanished, leaving nothing but crap. They could have afforded better, he thought, and he tried to let them know by thinking it hard and with directional intention toward the Pleiades, then past Andromeda where, he was afraid, the signal might be diffused among interstellar dust because he never got a check-sum. Blasting his thoughts into the multiverse apparently had little effect, compared to being in the Skein where even a dream resulted in realities. The Skein existed beyond the mental grasp of people on the planet, earth at a point in its space-time arc at which it was learning to mine energy-and-matter sufficiently to swarm into more of a hive, a collective called "humanity," but not knowing yet how much of one thing it all was, except as a thought, rarely an experience. The Skein had grown over eons, links and loops creating nodes so dense, they seemed to earthly eyes like smears. Their abilities were beyond the appearance of magic, they seemed like miracles. Cognitive artifacts distributed in the Skein in an open source manner enabled the manipulation of matter and energy at a level which if it was a rung on a ladder would be a thousand miles up, while earth was but a couple of feet off the ground. The Skein was a cornucopia of endless streams of frames spilling out of thousands of systems, billions of planets, trillions of stars, more than trillions of galaxies, woven into a net that transcended the flux which winked in and out and from which it had emerged. Energy became information, and time was understood "over time" to be elastic, so what they called "the future" here on earth could be seen to be a mold in the present. The multiverse worked within constraints that limited the apertures through which sentient life looked out (or in — language made it so difficult to think basic things like that) to see what was left in the light-dark mass that they could use like children using clay to fill in the rest — whatever was not yet themselves/ItSelf/OurSelf/the Skein.

Riding the bus as it rocketed across the frozen terrain, Jack savored the memories he could gather, dim and fading, of the Skein from whence he came, or so he believed, holding his origin as a fact, not a belief. Beliefs dissolved in the tyranny of time. Facts, however malleable, remained.

That was his story, and he was sticking to it. He arrived with a flash of light in the sagebrush desert not far from the Salt Lake City airport, his brain downsized to fit a human form. He was clothed and dewy-eyed and tried to collect himself as he inhaled the raw cool air of the planet in winter. He hated to lose access to the Skein, where he was part of All-in-All, and have to rely on transceiving signals as he could with an all-too-human brain. But that was the premise of the show. The series had a minimum number of episodes, already paid for, and a sketched-out narrative of (hopefully) hilarious encounters with humans. The future was waiting, and all he had to do was keep walking forward, learn a few lines and ad lib the rest. Always say "yes" to whatever was given. He just had to remember the arc, heading toward a finale roughed out in advance. He felt like Gordy Nelson running a perfect route until a pass landed in his hands. Anticipatory foresight of inevitable entanglements imprinted the present like footprints in mud, forms into which the liquid future was always oozing.

Memories, he reflected. We're talking about memories. Humans seem to believe them instead of knowing they were malleable and plastic They stayed or disappeared depending on their value for survival. Once they were gone — forget it. A few humans knew that but still lived as if, as if memories were an external frame, instead of a cage of their own making. Well, that made them cute, in a way, more innocent, thinking they were what they seemed to be to themselves.

So stay with the script, be as human as you can be, meet someone cute (he already had, and that would be Heidi! Check that box!), stay playful and remember, it's mostly humor, dude, with a few sad moments now and then for appropriate contrast. Keep it light, he thought or remembered he was told — he was already so human, he couldn't tell — and he smiled at the window, seeing his grin in front of the reflected face of the guy beside him who was twisting around a lot as Jack spoke aloud or smiled while looking at what he, his neighbor, could not see or spoke to voices that he, his neighbor, could not hear. Jack would be glad to explain, if asked, how he was tuned to different frequencies, but the guy never did. Most of the time, people don't, they just form judgments, and that's that. An incurious lot, all in all.

Jack could tell them whatever he liked about the Skein. No one would believe him. It would always sound crazy to native ears. Life in the Absolute Elsewhere would sound like slipstream, sci-fi, or a joke. Australopithecines were but glints in their mothers' eyes when galaxies first collapsed into one another and self-transcended toward the Skein. Better for the moment for humans to think they're the apple of some God's eye. The top of the food chain (that's a laugh!).

Secure in the snow globes in their heads, they swat away anomalies like flies.

Maybe stay with Utah, then, as a story of his origin. So a second rule he wrote with care was "no one must know" — which came from that same heroine, Mattie Walker-not-her-name. "Promise me, Ned. No one must know." — Teufel nodded, sitting on his bed in the Reindeer Motel , watching it again on the Iowa line, shivering in the chill but getting that what she said was important, getting the urgency of her concern, looking (if someone looked in the window through the curtains) like Gaear Grimsrud watching the soap when the woman cried, "I'm pregnant!" jerking the killer's chain in his cold lair.

Jack understood why a species must not know too much too soon. They all had to move up the ladder of self-awareness one identity at a time, including and transcending all that came before, taking the time to integrate, synthesize, and only then, self-transcend. Tell them too much, they wouldn't understand; tell them what they know, they would yawn. They have to move up by responding to challenges, not too easy not too hard, until they paused at what they always think is the end of the road for all time instead of a momentary break in an endless upward spiral. The Skein learned that too, over time, and the Bulk was littered with the remains of failed experiments. It was all dust in the solar winds, with plenty of time for the dust to become planets again when gravity made it clay again.

OK, he told himself for the umpteenth time, wear a human persona like a second skin and seem to be vaguely aware, a sleepwalker wandering down the aisle of a plane before an air marshal tackles his sorry Ambien-riddled ass. Then you'll blend in.

His initial task, and the rationale for all those stops in cheap motels, was to learn about humans by surfing the net, watching cable TV, seeing videos, reading a few books, graphic novels, magazines in waiting rooms, and reading the streets themselves. Streets were a kind of media too through which humans moved like rats in a maze. He had to learn the dialect of the tribe, the lingo of the streets. He listened to passengers and practiced conversations until his companions moved to another seat, which they did often, letting him try another. For Teufel, every disgusted glance as they left was an opportunity to learn, every scowl and curse a mark of progress.

Most videos, streamed at night in those motels, were entertaining. More than once his laughter made idiots in another room bang on his wall and shout "Shut the fuck up!" or its more polite equivalent, "Shut up, God damn you!" They often banged twice or a third time. Jack jumped with every thump, treating them as music. They sounded a lot to him like rap. He called back, "Hey! Fuck you too!" which he learned from HBO. He engaged with the other tenants the way the guy in "*Her*" learned to engage with the AI. He learned enough English to pretend to speak meaningfully. He practiced in convenience stores with clerks and later used Dade the same way, learning that baristas were taught to engage in cheerful chats to sell more coffee.

Humans were a funny species, all right. But — duh! — that's why he was there — to be a straight man and send encounters and conversations straight from his brain to repeaters in multiple dimensions. This was his first prime-time gig and he better not fuck it up. Based on feedback to the pilot, "Hello, Moroni!" — shouted like Robin Williams saying *Hello, Viet Nam!* — and the first episode, "Jack Rides the Bus" — the demographic was happy, and the twice-twisted twains were ecstatic. Tremenis and droots were a tougher sell — on earth, they probably watch *Jackass!* or *Idiocracy*. But most of the audience fused and seemed to be amused, lobes trembling, transceiving with glee, chortling like fools with their pants on the ground and hats turned around.

The success of the pilot only intensified his anxiety about staying alert in a human frame with an all-too-human body-brain. But he made a leap of faith and folded the ghosts of his Skeintime lateral lobes inward like leathery wings which made it difficult to remember who he had been, out there, but let him be more human and focus on the role.

Transceiving signals were emitted from "somewhere below, behind his ears" — how it felt to humans to begin to link. "It comes from below, behind, I guess," he told Heidi later, when she asked what he was doing, staring like that, his lips moving but nothing coming out. "I'm scanning," he said, "Sometimes I'm rehearsing. Or distributing raw feeds to the Skein." He tapped the base of his skull, on the outside, of course. "It comes from back here. It would look like iron filings in the shape of a butterfly if you could see it. But you can't."

"Oh," she said. "And you can?"

"Of course," he said. "But not in the way you mean. It's like that flavor, the one that's hard to say, edamame?"

"You mean umami?"

"Yes."

"Oh," she said, hitting a wall she would come to know intimately.

"Let me tell you, Heidi: if you could tune in, my scans would look like northern lights, multi-sensory wrap-arounds projected at neutrino-speed, rainbow-waves riding a bow-shock curve, edited to taste for a novelty-starved pan-galactic Skein that twitter like bats at twilight with delight."

"Oh," she said again. "I see. Of course."

His exchanges on the bus *were* pretty funny. Once a number of young men with brown bags in their hands boarded in a town with a prison. Jack chatted with several. He thought, if these people are typical, I will be king of this planet. They were dumber than a box of rocks. He interrupted their prattling — he couldn't help it — and said loudly several times, listening to their inane opinions, based on little or nothing, "Oh dear Christ!" Editors removed his comments and streamed the chats as teasers. The cosmos overflowed with bubbles of laughter and shrieks of glee. The show was on the road.

It became a real lark. Despite how much he hated the bus, he grew attached as one will to a prison cell, and he resisted when the bus arrived at his final destination. The busload of malodorous living things had turned into a lab for Jack. They did not burst into "Tiny Dancer" to unite the fractious tribe, but they swayed and rocked across the land with malice for all most of the time and on good days, indifference. They did their best to ignore one another while Jack did his best to engage in conversation. He was a born extrovert in a cage with engineers. He grew to love how hard it was, making sense of what humans said. The windblown snow blasted the windows, foggy portals framing a world covered with snow and ice. Dim light dawned late, persisted a bit, then faded early into darkness. Counting the hours, wishing the trip was over, they were humans on the move, barely linked, not even close to being looped, tucked in and snug in an overheated bus, their senses dulled by the hours and the miles, the monotony a perfect trigger to enter an altered state if only they knew how to use it.

CHAPTER 2
Good Morning, Moroni!

Monotony wearied the erstwhile traveler. One of the westerns he watched showed Indians wrapping a guy in rawhide, leaving him in the sun so the rawhide tightened. That's how Jack felt coming into a human form. His awareness of the cosmos, how vast it was, bursting with intelligence, an extended web becoming aware of itself like suns in galactic nurseries bursting into light, dissipated as he rode, the days short, the low clouds unbroken by sunlight except a teaser here and there, the seats on the bus so hard he was sure he would get a seatsore.

His brain felt stuffed into a thimble, spam in a can, as pilots said, dismissing the first astronauts.

To be human is to suffer, Jack wrote in his notebook, his handwriting made illegible by the bouncing of the bus. His connection to the Skein felt like a thin tendril, although like all sentience, he could never disconnect. But some days, it felt like he had.

Being human certainly had drawbacks. Humans think they're

separate from everything else which makes them sad, he thought, as if they're specks of dust, disconnected and alone. Who wouldn't feel bad, thinking that way? Thinking that a child's drawing of the cosmos, a few worlds and a handful of stars, is all there is?

The human mind is a prison cell, Jack thought morosely, the brain in solitary confinement, and after a while it hallucinates. If nothing's coming in, humans make it up. If dots are few, they connect them too soon. Then they share pictures and circle the wagons. The mirage becomes a skewed echo of the Skein.

As the days on the bus wore him down, his thinking grew foggy. Memories of dingy motels merged with the story of his false origins, growing up in a broken home in Salt Lake City, a site chosen for the low odds that anyone would know the locale (most Mormons stayed or returned from missions on which they were chained to each other like prisoners. The "Others" left as soon as they could). The features of rooms he rented on the road turned into memories of the small house in which he said he was raised.

"It felt like it was always cold. I could see the top of the spire through my bedroom window, looking west and south," he said suddenly, waking, for example, a female seatmate from a shallow doze. Her eyes blinked open and she wondered, what the fuck? "The angel, what's his name, Moroni? shines in the sun as Mormons think he did in life. I had few friends as a child — my parents were Jack Mormons, angry with all the bullshit, like the time my sister had to fuck a sheriff on the road to Antelope Island when she went to park with a guy named Russell. The cop scared them shitless when he turned on the spotlight and made her boyfriend sit in the prowler while he humped her, apparently a thing he did a lot, pulling up behind kids in the dark, which did get him arrested when a girl from Kaysville named LaPrell told her parents. But the fat bastard stood up in sacrament meeting and cried a while and said he was sorry so all was forgiven, no charges filed — I used the word "friends," but they weren't friends exactly, kids were told to avoid me by their parents. They said I was a danger because I was different. They wore these garments under their clothes and knew I didn't. God apparently told them to do that, so they'd know who was in, who was out. Like Jews and Moslems not eating pigs. I was out, obviously. I wore jeans and regular shirts from Goodwill. But hey, if one of the sects is right, Mormons or Catholics or Orthodox Jews or Evangelicals, the others must be wrong, right? Damned, I mean? Damned forever by a God who is obviously one vindictive hateful prick?" — his seatmate turning and looking at him, seeing what she expected, looking back the other way, thinking Jesus, my luck. "I heard from my parents how they abused kids and beat up women, then covered it up, a story you don't get in Reader's Digest, do you? The worst times were Valentines Day and the first day of deer hunting season. Then they confess, pay a tithe, tell the wife or kid to shut the fuck up, and that's that, like humans everywhere apparently, humans humans humans all the way down. I do not honestly know how you survived while bonobos fill the littlest niche."

The woman gripped her carry-on tightly, wrapping her arms around it, holding it close, stirring from her dreams. Her defenses, designed to ensure isolation and the sanctity of ideas derived from the air, from nothing at all, weren't working very well and she had to push back.

"What in hell are you talking about?"

"This is my story," Jack said. "How I got here. Why I find myself on the bus. I am practicing props to support my persona like all humans do. If I say it enough, I will believe it, and so will you. You are made to mistake the story for deeper things you cannot see. I am like a snake shedding skins. Yet somehow I remain the same, the snake inside abides. The landscape is littered with skins, but here I sit. It's a good trick your minds learned to play, picked up long before the neolithic, I would think. Before we came and tweaked your DNA."

She looked closely at what she decided was a complete idiot or a moron, hard to tell which. "Are you stoned? Are you batshit crazy? What the hell is with you, man?"

Jack laughed. "I wish I was stoned! No, I am as sane as the winter day is short. If I sound high, it is because of dislocation. I descended recently from the Skein. Although 'descend' is not exactly right. I downsized into a baby human body/brain, and the adjustment is non-trivial. Try it some time. Try to think, for example, like a dog, preferably a small one, a chihuahua for example."

"Well the days are long enough on this bus," she said, balancing her bag on her lap, looking to see where he had his hands, making sure he wasn't stealing things or trying to grope her. "And besides, I knew Mormons in Idaho. I lived in Pocatello for ten years. They were good neighbors. They had my back. Jesse never hit his wife. So what the fuck are you talking about?"

Jack smiled. "Thank you for sharing. When you contest my narrative, you know, you give it credibility, like UFOogists who know nothing debating one another. Then people think there are real sides. Still, my story is credible, yes? I am still practicing, so please, give me a break. I sound sincere, don't I? As sincere as a dog? — have you ever known a dog to be insincere? Dogs do not know how to lie, do they?"

"I don't know shit about dogs and lies. Don't people say, let a sleeping dog lie?"

Teufel laughed. "How does a sleeping dog lie, in its dreams? Think for a minute: can you imagine a dog wagging its tail, licking your hand, then going for your throat?"

"No. You're describing politicians, not dogs."

Jack wrote that down. It might be useful in the upper Midwest city to which he was headed.

"Thank you for that insight. Well — since you are awake, would you like to listen to more of my story?"

"Oh, sure," she said, she hoped with sufficient irony, and snorted, turning away, staring across the aisle at a couple coupling under a blanket. She watched their humps and bumps as they did whatever they did, making little noises now and then, one of the heads popping up like someone under water, gulping air, then going down another time. Jack took her silence as assent and talked to her back, trying out scenarios, all that David Copperfield crap, how he was raised in a "dysfunctional" family, as all human families were, one way or another, more or less. "Nevertheless, I survived," he insisted, humming I will survive, mostly to himself. "Like most human children, I was bent, I was like a pretzel inside, but I learned how to live. I did my best to make life around me conform to my twisted shape. I had to get out of that valley, of course, not being LDS, so here I am, I am escaping the tangled skein — a skein in a bad way, I mean — and heading for the Midwest. I am no more warped or distorted than most. It's a good story, yes? I can't change reality but I can change the facts." — he laughed when he said that, sprinkling spittle onto the back of her dark parka.

She kept herself turned away as best she could, constrained by the arms of the narrow seat, her face to the aisle. She tried to go to sleep again but his chattering interfered. At the next stop, Louella (for that was her name) hurried to another seat the minute someone left, and then this tall guy got on, his hair disheveled, eyes rheumy, pores exhaling the stale stink of drink. After hearing Jack for a bit, he looked for a different seat too. Nothing was available. So he staggered up the aisle to talk to the driver, holding the sides of seats along the way, gesturing back at Jack, his face making the case, but the driver shook his head, saying, the man bugs you, sit somewhere else. The guy glared at the driver, saying, Fuck, man! The only empty seat is a shelf on top of the goddamn engine. It's fucking hot, and you can't lean back — oh fuck it, man, whatever.

"Yes sirree," said the driver, used to dealing with half-wits and fools. "I don't care what you do. Just sit down. You can't stand in the aisle. "

The guy said, fuck you, paused, then added another "fuck you," getting in the last one to tighten his argument a bit, then made his way to the back, giving Jack a look as he passed — a-ha! Jack got it. The man was upset: good, that was useful feedback — and the guy flopped in the only open seat, over the motor like he said, where he sat stiffly, looking like Lily Tomlin with her legs hanging down, his feet unable to reach the floor.

The route they mapped for Jack had lots of stops. They had him tacking back and forth across his destination, giving him time to practice, arriving at last in the city in which he left the bus with a headache caused by using his new brain in its cute little bone-plate skull with very little give a bit too much. The sense of a larger identity in the Skein, embedded in the Foam as it winked in and out, where he had heard the snap crackle and pop of the froth of intelligent sentience co-extensive with everything-- that had sadly faded to a wisp. By the time he was walking with the woman named Heidi down a snowy crowded street, he no longer thought of himself as a bubble in the Foam, and he couldn't hear a thing from the Skein. All he detected was static and maybe a faint signal now and then, or what he thought was a signal, he couldn't tell, becoming more human than he liked.

So he fell back on local feeds — email, tweets, things like that — and diverse nodes — phones, pads, laptops, even the few remaining "newspapers," using local names for nodes — as back-ups to the stream from the center that he deeply missed. And once in a while, the signal did come through, so he knew he wasn't completely nuts.

Coming up the stairs of the bus station that morning, he could still smell the humans wrapped in their warm clothing, stewing in their juices, a pretty bad stench. He looked up at the sky between the platform and the entrance hall and inhaled the cold air, hoping to freshen his palate. An overcast sky like the lights of the city at night made seeing stars impossible. Living in civilization was like having cataracts, even if he saw the "Milky Way," which was invisible at that latitude, he wouldn't be able to see it. Besides, it was one of the cloudiest months of the year, and the stars wouldn't look like nodes in a network but like points of light, like silver jacks flung into a cloud.

He trudged up the stairs from the platform, his backpack bumping his sore back, into the dim entrance hall. He paused at the top of the stairs, squinting in the dim light, his arrival in the city a lot different than his manifestation in the intermountain west with a flash of light and hope in his heart.

When he popped out in Utah, he found himself behind a juniper tree surrounded by three-tip, fuzzy and black tip sage. Had a human seen him, they would have turned what was literally unthinkable into an image of a vehicle settling slowly onto the desert with a motion like a falling leaf. They would invent details to make their story real, filling in the blanks. They would find indentations in the sand where pods set down, they would discover burnt leaves in a circle, they would see small humanoids rushing to the "ship." But as it happened, no one saw, no one heard. A truck was the nearest vehicle and it was heading west at highway speed, the driver in a trance.

In fact, Jack had arrived through a tear in the fabric of space-time itself, a slit in the Bulk made by prying it open, liberating light (ionizing the air around the weak force, in fact) which would have blinded anyone who looked to what was going on. The light was so white, they would say, describing ionization, not the thing inside, what they thought they saw, it was so white, whiter than any white I ever saw.

He arrived in a yellow and black plaid jacket and flappy leather hat. He climbed a fence and walked down the road toward the city. Someone came by in a car and asked if he wanted a ride. Jack waved them on, getting used to the air and the city ahead floating along the mountains like a cloud. There was snow on the tops of the mountains and houses lower down on the slopes. It was in the forties with filtered sunlight in the valley, and there were strip malls and car lots along the road. He looked closely at desert scrub and sharp-edged sage, enjoying the minty odor in the air and the intense light reflected from the leaves. The yellow dwarf they called "the sun" smoldered in the hazy sky. The streets were wide and empty compared to ones he saw on Google maps in the Midwest city.

He headed for the Temple, knowing it was near the station

from which he would leave. But first he would patrol the streets, committing the grid to memory. As he walked, he stored details, made up stories of kids not letting him play, going to the ward for scouts where they tried to recruit him, having dates with a few Gentile girls. He dreamed up one named Carla on whose soft belly he came for the first time at fourteen before she showed him how to slip inside, pretending he was the first. He tried to imagine how it felt, his penis sliding in for the first time, and he couldn't even guess. The movies that showed things like that were shot from the outside, and all they showed was a guy as he gasped or made an excited noise. He studied how their breathing changed, how easily a woman or a male partner if they liked it like that could play them like a piccolo, using teeth gently now and then to elicit a stronger gasp. But until he slid his dick into a slippery slot, the feeling would elude his grasp.

He filled the Salt Lake City streets with memories of accidents, buildings exploding, movie scenes, dialog from Grand Theft Auto. Pretty soon his head was an imaginary landscape of mean streets as vivid and as real as the virtual streets down which the hacker, Don Coyote, rode in the night, righting egregious wrongs.

In his jacket pocket was a key to a locker at the Greyhound station. He went there and found a knapsack with things he needed for the trip. He knew there were cameras everywhere so he acted like a native, incurious and aloof, and sat on a bench in the station and closed his eyes and waited for the bus.

The bus station smelled like a mammal dump. People wandered around in the odorous haze, oblivious to their reek. By the time he left Salt Lake, sitting halfway back in the bus at a window on the right, his yellow-and-black jacket buttoned up and the flaps on his hat snapped, he was used to the smell. He learned to filter air through his nose, using hairs evolved for that purpose. Walking beside Heidi in the night, his first night in town, he opened his nostrils wide, inhaling her scent, a smell of soap that had lathered her body that morning mixed with odors of the street - cold stone, sublimating snow, fumes from cars and buses. The air smelled as if it were on fire. The auto exhaust filled the sky like smoke, illuminated by holiday lights. But through it all her perfume snaked its wily way, tickling him and making his dick twitch. He wanted her at once, then and there, he wanted to fuck.... what was her name... Heidi... "Heidi," he said aloud, "I am ready, Heidi, ho.

"I am ready to rumble."

"What?" she said.

"I am ready," he said.

She looked at him askance. "Ready for what?"

"You tell me. The woman determines it I think, in the end. Whatever. Whenever."

Heidi laughed, amused by his somewhat cutesy oddness. Wounded men were her thing all right, she smelled them a mile away and reeled them in without thinking. Then they flopped in her net until her lack of give-and-take became cloying, her give-alone as destructive as it was protective. They tried to negotiate, but it never worked, then they ranted, trying to crack her with brute force, then they gave up and left.

"OK," she said. "Whatever."

"Good!" he said, thinking that sealed the deal. His template for a sexual adventure came from *Grays*, *Girls* and *Sex in the City* so he knew it took maybe ten minutes before people threw off their clothes and began to fuck wherever they were, in the day room, in a fire station, on the floor, in a washroom on a plane, joining some club. He smiled, glad he had done his homework, learning to stop at pancake's house (his name for the pause before the fuck) before finding a bimbo who could ring his tinkling bells.

He tried *The Bridges of Madison County* to learn other approaches but it was so smarmy and sick-witted, he couldn't make it through. He cleansed his palate by binge-watching *Laverne and Shirley* in Cedar Rapids, eating pizza on the bed, thin and crispy with sausage and mushroom and extra cheese from Marco's in a strip mall near the motel that kindly slipped a menu (red white and black) under his door. It was near a sub shop and a telephone store and a nail place, an interesting way to arrange stores, Teufel thought, all in a row.

He read a few books too. He liked Nick Adams. When he read about his fishing trip, he tried to understand how things could be inside a man that a man could not say but could feel deeply and truly and which, somehow, the reader felt deeply and truly. He read how his hands trembled as he tied a fly and inferred the nature of human wars — jigsaw pieces fitting into a pattern of how they began (by mistake or design), filled themselves with battles and burials, screams and salutes, and ended with medals and dead heroes, a few borders changing as the planet took a breath before the next war.

It's not easy, he wanted to tell Heidi, getting used to life on a planet out in a spiral arm on the edge, space-time lagged and culture shocked, sluggish of wit and bone-cold to boot in this goddamned wind. But he said nothing, walking beside the woman he had picked up as a prop — a handy randy woman, a palliative of sorts, a healer of his loneliness, looking at him now in the lights of passing traffic and the brightly lighted windows with a smile, her lips pale in the harsh light: Heidi in the twilight, a dark blue woolen cap on her head, the dark sky behind, buildings higher than the sky, the wintry city frozen in its purpose, whatever that might be, not as random as it seemed, Teufel hoped.

He gingerly pushed the flaps onto his ears — cute, she thought, his oak pale hair thinner, whiter than she expected, coming out from under the hat as he made it snug. That gesture, pushing in the flaps, then wincing as he turned into the wind, struck her as cute too. His face reflected the light; the tips of his fingers were cold, growing numb.

"You need gloves," Heidi said.

He grinned again as if he had just remembered (which he had). Duh! He dug a pair from his pocket, turning into the shelter of a doorway to work his stiff fingers into the stiff fingers.

"If it fits, you must acquit," he said, pleasing himself, flexing his fingers in the leather, pleasing Heidi too, it seemed, for she laughed and touched his arm lightly the way some women did, with a hint of intimacy, an implicit promise, perhaps, or more likely, he thought, manipulative control, trying to tame him with a transparent strategy. He was proud of himself for learning that from romcoms. *Look at the big brain on Jack!* — hell, he felt good (he remembered Adam Lambert, pausing on the stairs, singing "I feel good" in that great sexy gay way), and what the hell, Jack thought, he felt great, in fact, surfing a sudden rush, high on a lack of sleep and cultural distortion.

He smiled in the darkness, thinking he understood this woman pretty well, and all women, really, all Americans, in fact, reminding himself that these were mostly Americans around him, this odd lot flowing up and down the street, surging from offices, banks, and stores into the winter night like characters in a pop-up book, one in which he too had just popped up, in color and three dimensions, blissful after endless dull gray 2-D days on the suffocating bus.

That Heidi might be a little clueless, that was good. Her naiveté like her fragrance tickled him featherlike inside. It was — cute, that innocence, fresh and primitive. It might be something humans would keep as they took the reins of evolution into their own hands. Thousands of years earlier, his forebears had spawned reflective selves by tweaking genes, enabling a tribal life and brains big enough to manage it through a honeycomb of co-extensive memories, storing data in brains, growing more lobes, creating a fractalized mirage of cloud-based data resident in short-term storage in their flesh. Then they learned how to store information and memories outside too, striving to reach for a place in the Skein. Unfortunately, they damn near trashed the planet and now teetered on the brink — but hey, he thought, who gives a flying fuck? — a phrase he heard a lot on HBO and an easy phrase to say since Jack had plenty of human fuck-you code inside him, too.

He thought of how most of those around him imagined the multiverse. There was a big yellow moon, then Mars, a couple of gas giants, a handful of stars, a nearby galaxy, then light diffused to the end of their narrow perspective: the human view from the bottom of the deep well of night. But only for the moment. As parents said to kids during a bad time, often in adolescence, "if you just don't kill yourself over [fill in the blank], you'll be a great adult." Just hang in and hang on.

The same for the whole planet. Fifty fifty, pretty iffy. But if they did:

One day you will see the universe.

He laughed, wondering when. Heidi looked sideways toward

his chuckling, wondering something else. He noticed her glance and thought, OK, use your brain: engage with lower level thinking. Throttle back *fast* and adapt to the pace of this cute human.

"Thinking of something funny," Jack said.

He laughed again, and Heidi to keep him company laughed a little too, with him or at him, he didn't know which and didn't care. Her laughter sounded like silver bells in contrast to the jangling of a Salvation Army skank in the shelter of a doorway shaking a hand bell, making people look — hey, look at me! — her dark blue red-rimmed hood pulled tight around her tighter smile. She wanted money, he could see, which was why she was clanging the bell. Give me money! Why? Because I embody the narrative of Christmas as a come-on. So cross my palm with gold.

He heard her say "have a nice day" to the back of a man who was walking away indifferent to her pitch — her way of saying, "Hey, fuck you, you cheap prick." But some must have bought her bullshit because they jangled coins into her metal bucket, getting "thank you" in response. That was the pay-off, reciprocity a binding glue easy to manipulate.

He smiled again, delighted that his mind was working so well, as Heidi he would learn later was delighted with the first long sip of a mango lassi before hot samosas came down on a plate in a waiter's hands. Heidi, across the table, radiating pleasure. Perhaps she was thinking of Indian food then. His invisible antennae beat the air, picking up her hunger, but not its source which was somewhere inside where he couldn't reach. She was hungry, he felt, for more than food. Maybe she wanted Jack to fill her up. Maybe she was lonely too. Loneliness seemed to be axiomatic to humanity like an itch they could never scratch. But that made it potent: it spurred them to strive to form a hive.

A primitive precursor of the entire Skein.

He made an effort to focus on data from his senses. He noticed songs coming from speakers decorated with wreaths and angels, the sweet noels a counterpoint to Heidi's felicitous giggle. That made him remember music streaming from an idiot's ear buds behind him on the bus. The girl made strange noises too, thinking she was singing. She sounded wounded, moaning unintelligibly, audible enough to be annoying. The tap of her hand on her knee and a kick now and then to the back of his seat made him simmer for one hundred sixty two miles, building to a rage, until they were leaving one more nameless town, a few lights before the darkness of the fields began, and he had had it up to here (he gestured toward his neck, inside) and whirled in his seat and screamed at the hollow-eyed girl, "Turn that shit down! Turn it the fuck down!"

Her cow eyes widened. He must hate her, she felt, he thought, and in accordance with the principle of reciprocity, she hated him back. He felt it and doubled down, hating her even more. Which made her hate him back more. Their mutual contempt threaded their silent stare-down — there was nothing else to do on the bus, anyway — until he was about to backhand her into the middle of next week, which she must have picked up for she suddenly twisted in her seat, fidgeting to find a button on the thing, squirming into a where-is-the-goddamn-volume sort of shape while maintaining a sideways fuck-you look, but she did turn it down, she did turn the goddamn music the fuck down and sit back and stare at the window at her own reflection as if he didn't exist and as if she hadn't gone down to a shameful ignominious defeat.

"Thank you." he said. "Jesus fucking Christ!"

Pouring syrup on the pancakes of victory.

That image lingered in his mind. He wondered, walking beside this softer gentler Heidi, if it might have been better to choose a persona that was... well, more moderate. Less thin-skinned, perhaps. Less angry, less intense. He didn't know. Maybe they loaded him up with too much T. Well, time would tell, he thought, his rear foot dragging (metaphorically speaking) behind him in the dark stars from which he came, behind the stars invisible in the cold night, obscured by the glow of the city, his awareness reaching beyond the winter skies to multiple intersecting origami-like dimensions of a cosmos those around him couldn't see. And if he told them, using local frames of reference, they wouldn't understand, like Semmelweis telling doctors to wash their hands.

And you, Jack, are also sort of human. Remember that! You are Jack Teufel (that was the gentleman's name, an unusual name, which Heidi had to think to remember, then remember to think — Teufel Teufel Teufel she said, giving it a hook on which to hang like an ornament on her Christmas tree, which she had in fact decorated earlier that week, her once-alive-now-very-dead sparkly tabletop "holiday" tree — no, she answered her own question, hearing herself ask on behalf of this or that friend, no she was not being politically correct, that was just how she was, like a Buddhist — thinking her tree was already dropping needles in the heat, the air in her apartment more arid than the desert. Seeing herself (in her mind's eye) sweep them from the hardwood floor into a dustpan with a whisk broom, then slide from the pan to a garbage can. Smelling orange rinds, coffee grounds, hearing the clang of the metal top bang back onto the pail. Seeing the tip of her fashionable black boot sliding from the pedal.

Then she was back beside him on the street.

He smelled oranges and coffee grounds too. But then forgot. Because it didn't link.

She repeated his name, "Teufel," moving her lips, and slipped her arm into his, skipping a bit to keep pace with his quicker step. He heard her whispering to herself as she hurried beside him, sliding on a patch of slick, and he looked down at her slipping feet in fashionable black boots, the ones into which as he waited Heidi had changed before leaving the kiosk, Teufel leaning on the counter and practicing waiting patiently for a woman as men often had to do as she removed her powder blue sneakers and white socks over dark tan pantyhose which she layered, she explained, because there was a draft in the station, pulling boots up one at a time, then pushing her feet down to make them snug, her feet now sliding on dry cold trampled snow. But she stayed steady, holding his arm, keeping up and wondering what she was doing, hurrying through a rush-hour crowd with a guy just off the bus, a cipher to whom she had already sort of connected, sort of attached — and not only what was she doing, but why?

Well, she knew why, sort of. Because she was trying to trust her intuition, that's why. Dr. Gillespie had encouraged her to follow the crumbs through the forest of her life before they were eaten by birds. What's the worst that could happen? he asked. Heidi shrugged. Not much, she guessed. Correct, said the sage with a smile, looking up into her eyes (he was four inches shorter, even when Heidi wore flats). Not much.

Behind them, when they had left the station, the big glass door had closed slowly and a big uniformed cop hurried to slip in before it shut. Teufel paused, amazed at the size of the guy. He imagined him beating a perp with a telephone book. Maybe using a taser, dropping him like a sack. He had seen those scenes on TV so many times it was like they were facts.

Other cops on the sidewalk milled about to keep warm, a lot of those huge bastards hanging out, more than he expected. Maybe the mayor was around. Maybe they were looking for terrorists. It was big business, watching everyone. The cops looked cold too, hats pulled down, coats buttoned up. Another one, even bigger than the first, a massive guy, what with his stun guns, chemical sprays, a club and gun on a thick belt around his Brobdingnagian bulk, kept touching one gloved knuckle to his eyes to blot tears from the cold. He looked like the guy in the sixties poster giving his finger to the world. He did in fact look like a pig, Teufel thought, remembering the chants in the angry streets, he had the eyes perhaps of a fascist bastard ready to kick whoever was down, which he had learned was what they all did. Ears, snout, everything — Teufel learned so much from cable — so now, when an image fit, it snapped into place in his brain like a plastic bead, building a virtual world in which he lived.

Wait! Who was thinking that, about the police, that they were pigs? Was it Heidi or Jack?

For a moment he didn't know. Information was leaking nonlocally, that he knew, brain to brain, brane to brane, the distance between them both short and irrelevant. It was not electromagnetic, after all. Distance did not seem to matter when the data rearranged itself. Heidi and Jack were physically close, yes, while he and his director were in different systems, different galaxies in fact, but it all winked in and winked out, sustained somehow, and information might be connected to anywhere, everywhere, a noospherical sort of thing, and in this dimension, at their stage of development, without a balloon above a head to say who was thinking what, without a graphic novel based on his narrative (one he was sure would be written in a few years) — pigs, thinking police were pigs, that had to be Teufel, not Heidi. Heidi never thought of cops or anyone else as pigs. She noticed the cops, too, of course, big guys in blue uniforms, storing the image, then forgetting it, her brain rating it "unimportant." Teufel stayed with his image, however, his fear of police indelible after engaging with all that media. His lips moved, telling an imaginary cop to fuck off, raising his hands to ward off the blow that was sure to come. He had no idea how he looked, raising his hands, fending off imaginary threats. Nor did most humans, living defensively, protecting themselves from threats that never came. His fear segued into anger, setting off sparks like a welding torch.

Now, Heidi had "the gift," Dr. Gillespie never tired of telling her, holding her by the shoulders and looking for a long while into her eyes before speaking, so she felt Jack's anger and fear as pressure at her temples, but she lacked the content, she sensed the field, but not the specifics. She had no point of reference, having just met him at the station that morning, for linking his feelings to what they might mean. When she thought of cops, she thought of protectors, shepherds keeping the wolves away. She was not a hater, she was quick to forgive, which made her ripe for subtle abuse but great for certain relationships, from some guys' points of view. But hey, give me a break, she thought, she was working on that, going to groups, learning to be assertive, more in charge of her own life, that kind of thing, reading Melody Beatty, and because she liked this new guy and wanted to like him more, her feelings about him, when they did flicker negatively, faded fast, because she did not want them to interfere with her wish for just one that worked out and did not devolve into one more codependent nightmare. Her brain was small, but just as effective at making frames and living in them as his. So she barely etched a memory of his behavior into short term storage before it disappeared.

She did notice that he slowed and looked back as if to see if someone was following. He searched the crowd for someone calibrated to their pace. His alarms were triggered by fear. He saw nothing suspicious, however. He looked ahead: No one waited in doorways. No one lingered, seeming to look in windows. But he wanted to be sure and stopped walking and turned toward a window into which he seemed to look, staring in fact without seeing anything, facing forward but his focus angled askance of his window-watching stance in a trance. Heidi stood in the bright light unselfconsciously and looked at big colorful puppets building toys, elves wrapping packages, angels on wires ascending in cotton clouds. (She didn't know if angels were real or not. The jury was out on that one. She had friends who went both ways. She hoped to ask Gillespie what he thought) — that's what she was thinking, thinking he was delighted by the display, and were angels a metaphor or real, and if they were real, was it angels that showed up at Gillespie's or were those discarnate beings of another kind? — while Teufel was focused not on elves or the animated Santa going ho-ho-ho at the back of the display but on reflections of people passing behind them on the walk. He looked for a pattern. The few cops remaining in ghostlike reflections in the glass looked like manatees. They were huge, their reflections floundering down the street, making Heidi and Jack look thin.

The analytical part of his brain traced the behavior of the crowd. It looked random. It looked like what humans did when what they call "work" was over and they escaped to a warm well-lighted refuge to drink and dull the memories of dull days. Nobody knew who he was. He was just another guy about whom passing people did not give a flying fuck. If they were thinking, they were thinking as usual of themselves.

He ended his surveillance and turned from the window and walked north, good little Heidi heeling.

"I love those windows," she said.

"Yes," he said. "Full of puppets. Angels. An obese white male called Santa."

The wind had grown stronger, drawing his attention to his stinging cheeks, dripping nose, tearing eyes. While focused on the imaginary threat, he shut out whatever his senses detected. Returning to normal modes, he felt, saw, smelled, and heard but did not quite touch the world. He felt as if his fingertips touched the glass in which it was encased. He jerked the back of his jacket down, looking again from windows of the department store to the crowd across the street and the dense traffic. He heard honking horns, saw the exhaust billowing in bright headlights. Then he caught more of Heidi's scent. The wind must have shifted, and her perfume exploded in his nose. He learned later it was called "Dusk." The street was suddenly luminous with her fragrance. His nostrils twitched, he licked his lips, an erection sprang to life. He knew then and there that he must fuck this woman. His mind brimmed with the image, he sniffed the rank ripe odor of her sex, licking her clit in his mind with gusto, while Heidi cried out and begged, yes, yes, now Jack, yes, and he felt himself slide inside and drive in to the hilt. His hips twitched, making him slip on the walk, as his dick did a little dance against the worn denim as if to say, *do it! do it!*. Meanwhile people flowed around them, a river of humanity in a rush, he and Heidi a quiet island, everyone else nothing but negative space.

Christmas music piping from a calliope enhanced the imaginative foreplay. He saw himself, felt himself, biting her nipple until she squeaked.

She must feel it, he thought. Then he thought:

The world is a chorus line, the pair of them up front, singing and dancing in top hats, tapping canes. The Heidi and Jack Show, leaving the station, hitting the road.

He looked at traffic which barely moved —"rush hour" they called it. They didn't know how to smooth out the rhythms of mechanized life. They clogged the pipes of their own civilization. — and suddenly, apropos of nothing, mild depression closed in. But he caught himself, hauling himself up by the nape of his neck. He was tired, he thought. That's all. And he was here, here at last, and Heidi was smiling under her cute blue hat as the streetlight under which she passed cast a slanting shadow across her face. She glanced in the direction of his internal mind-raking noise. He smelled her scent again which patterned the opaque darkness with patches of color like harlequin clothes. Her scent was silver red and blue. It made a musical sound. The silver trill rippled in the light, the cityscape of buildings growing dark, illuminated however with lighted windows all around. Twilight deepened, a deeper blue, as if construction paper had been pasted between buildings down the disappearing streets. The glare was electric, a recent technology on earth, illuminating snowy streets, women exhaling clouds of breath, and he saw, he felt it all. A young woman, her cheeks rosy in the cold, hurried past. She bumped his arm and turned with an apologetic smile and his heart pounded. There were all these women! They were every fucking where. *We don't know if there's a God but we know there are women.* He looked at Heidi, twinkling, and resolved again to bed her soon. Her arm was hooked in his, walking beside him as if they were a pair; oh, but he wanted to make her fingers grip and flex in the sheets as he thrust out of range of the camera from behind.

Her fragrance vanished suddenly in the wind. He smelled suddenly nothing but the cold stone buildings along which they walked, the snow-covered sidewalk. Nothing but winter. The night a bell jar, a hollow world. And they were all alone, inside.

Get some sleep, he told himself. Then sent his attention into the world.

Exhaust still filled the air, buses braked with a fingernail-on-blackboard screech. Autos crept forward, stopped, the smell of gas everywhere. He thought of the small towns through which the bus had plunged like a porpoise escaping an orca, tiny lights on a map in his mind, a grid that flexed like a view looking down on a simulation in a game. He worked hard to make his new life feel real, "This is the upper Midwest. I am in America. I am on the planet earth," he said aloud, and Heidi, hearing him, agreed.

"That's all true," she said. "No questions there."

He felt the rumbling bus rides vibrating in his body, the grooved pavement as he came into the city. The day was already stale when it opened, dawn already oppressive. The winter, he feared, would never end. Spring would never come. Anxiety made his breathing shallow. Heidi picked it up, thinking, maybe it was her, thinking, why do I make guys feel that way? as if she made him be what he was. What's wrong with me? she asked for the hundredth time. Then she wondered, would they sync? would they be friends? Fuck-buddies? Would they perhaps even… marry? and have children?

Was Jack the one to meet on the Empire State? Was he

Neo? Was Jack... The One?

She knew the universe brings people together, *Sleepless in Seattle*-like, it knows what people need — and wow! she thought, because in that very instant, while she was thinking those things, they did sync, they calibrated frequencies.

Maybe he made it happen, knowing she needed a sign. He moderated his pace, slowed so she wouldn't have to work so hard to walk beside him. He must have felt, she thought, that he needed a gal like her to throttle the agitation in his brain, and he adjusted at precisely that moment to her need for him to slow down. And he did feel something, not as if an airplane hit an air pocket and dropped, not exactly, but as if his feet were suddenly solidly on the ground and it was high fives all around, as if he was part of the crowd in a bar after a touchdown, after a few beers, as if he belonged on the planet.

His brief depression had lifted. His anxiety was gone.

He looked up at high rises all around, tall towers defining the frame in which they walked with planes of light, arranging their world. The landscape was contained, the city illumined, intelligent by design. And Heidi was thinking, calibration came because angels or spirits or discarnate guides or what some called "God," collapsing the lower levels into a single point at the top, linked their link to a larger link, to a loop, making it all cohere. Whatever the ultimate cause (as if humans can grasp that), Jack was calmer, rantless for the moment. Something had shifted. He felt it too. He looked at her face in the street light and gave her the smile, the one she was coming to like, and he took her hand in its knitted mitten and worked his fingers as best he could between hers, squeezing. She liked that, and she liked the way he angled his body in a complimentary way as if they already fit, as if they had known one another more than a few hours, as if the universe really was a mother and they were in its loving arms.

In other words, Teufel slowed a bit, and Heidi walked a little faster. Sixty forty, perhaps. But that was enough.

This could work, Heidi thought.

This could work, Teufel thought.

Yes, they thought. *This could work.*

Whatever they meant by "this" and "this" and — especially — "this."

CHAPTER 3
The Man Behind the Curtain

Heidi and Jack met cute on a cold windy day in a deep and dark December. She popped up out of the faceless mass minutes after Jack arrived. He stopped in his tracks, then headed for the kiosk. It was like a camera moving through the crowd, framing her with a customer, remaining on her face, letting her expressions play.

He told her he came from out west, but never told her why he left. That was a blank to be filled another day, she thought. Give him space. She asked if he was LDS. He laughed and said, "no, Jesus, I mean, no, I am not LDS," then laughed some more, shaking his head. "They are *weird*," he added, but then said seriously, "of course, I bet you would think my origins are weirder than *that*."

"Oh?" Heidi said. "The more I listen to people, the more I think everybody comes from a weird place. Even when they don't know. Maybe especially when they don't know, because they bought the story. They got into the frame and never left."

"They bought the bullshit!" Jack's face brightened like a bulb on a slider switch. "Yes, I agree."

"Where *are* you from?"

He smiled and winked. "Some say Utah. Some do not. I will tell you later, if it fits in the script. When the pupil is ready, I will teach. So come back in oh, a hundred thousand years, when the gene pool is more useful."

He gave her the grin.

"OK, sure, I'll do that," Heidi said. She was used to the way men took the high ground with that leaning-back-over-the-edge sort of look and let it bounce by like a well-hit ball to the wall. She didn't much care where he was from or what he had done or left undone. She knew he would tell her soon enough, if they kept hanging out. Men do tell in the end, without prompting, once sex makes them more pudding-like. It's all in the timing. The way to control the world, she was learning in her support group, was to let things take their course. Stay soft and pliable, adapt her shape to the shape of the day, or the guy, or the way it was, and wait. Above all, use epic sex to elicit information in the brief moment afterward, before the well filled up again.

She knew that people left things for all kinds of reasons. Lots of times they didn't know themselves, not until later when it didn't matter. Like accountability for egregious crimes by say the CIA, people find out after it doesn't matter any more, when perps are no longer in office, or dead, or can count on a pardon. Artichoke or Bluebird for example. Up against the truth of which, really, what chance cuddlies, as the man said? The question did not even have to be answered.

Doctor G taught that people made up stories called "my life" to support who they wanted to be and what they wanted to do.

They change them only when they can't stand it any more. "That's what therapy is," he explained, suggesting he might be of help, always trolling for new clients, "it's a way of rearranging data to release a different energy.

"So denial is your friend," he reassured Heidi when she thought she was missing the big picture. "Your psyche will let you know when it's OK to know. Otherwise it waits. Trust your Self, trust your psyche, as a guide."

That was easier to do, Heidi found, as she moved toward middle age, acting less impulsively, having some experience. She was, in addition, in good shape for a woman her age. She had left a few persons, places, times of life herself — she was moving from a time of life now, she thought, about to release the trapeze and fall, hoping the other bar would slap her hand. That's why, she decided, she was open to hooking up with a guy she didn't know. During transitions, when life felt like the ocean and she had lost a holdfast on the seabed, floating up freely into the dense kelp, she was open to the unexpected, sensitive to signs, trying to see what was coming so she could align with it. Something always arrived, which she called "what was coming," looking back, and the view from the new plateau became a benchmark for "normal." Soon she would not even remember how she looked at the world before because everything folded neatly into how it looked now. Origami folds that she thought were making a crane turned out to be making a UFO.

Why is it always a surprise? she asked Doctor G. It always makes sense, after the fact, but I never see it coming. It seems like wasted time, she said. Dr. Gillespie always smiled and took her hands in his and told her no, oh no, my dear, we can never see a new paradigm inside the old. It takes what it takes, and it takes time. Time is how we traverse the information we assess. Have you not seen *Interstellar*? Time is the binding on associations, the edge as it were, that links the links.

Heidi resisted, saying maybe she could see it if she tried hard enough. No, he would say gently, his thumbs stroking the tops of her soft hands, making slow circles, we can't, you see, being human. We are locked in body-brains that need what we call time to add those new threads to the weave.

Heidi shrugged and said well, maybe, you might be right — again (they both laughed) - and I admit that reasons pop into my mind only after the fact. Before, I don't have a clue — her mind's eye watched him smile, a point on a line of time that morphed into an image of Jack. Jack's face was more vivid, being more present now. She had no idea why, that cold morning, she watched him cross the hall from the stairs, his duffle bag bouncing on his back, obviously quite heavy, his expression off a bit as he trundled toward her, shifting the backpack as he did, searching for a better way to carry his burden, she thought, a metaphor she bet for his life, the guy standing out because of the yellow-and-black plaid jacket and flappy hat and funny grin. He was not exactly funny looking, although he wasn't circumcised, she learned later, but he definitely did look… different. His face expressed a different way of framing the world, and that was interesting to her, the right password to bypass her firewall or crypto and get in, and by the time she told the story of their meeting to Women Who Love Too Much Anon which she had attended faithfully for seventeen months, and called her sponsor as needed, and read the material many times until she knew it by heart, it was too late to change.

"It's never too late to change," said Nita, one of the informal leaders. She was a woman in her thirties struggling with her weight. She was going to OA too and thinking of adding another.

"In theory, no," Heidi concurred. "In practice, though?"

Standing behind the counter, shifting from foot to foot as the day made her legs ache, elbows on the glass where pipes and tobacco and bongs were displayed, she sized up the guy heading for the kiosk. I bet he buys nothing, Heidi thought. That means, I better decide, before he arrives, will I engage or not?

She read people well, even at a distance, without an introduction. You are so intuitive, Dr. Gillespie told her — Dr. James John Gillespie, Esquire, a minister of sorts, a therapist of sorts, his transactions with his voluntary tutees defining his value in old age. When he had something important to say, as he did that day, he paused, his hands on her shoulders which were hard to grasp when she wore that pink sweater with the embroidered lamb and pearls for eyes through which he could felt her skin, holding her shoulders and sort of massaging her upper arms, holding her gaze while she waited for his wise words. Heidi, he said, listen now: Heidi, my dear, you are not merely intuitive, you are an intuitive. <he paused > Heidi, you have a gift. You are special. Use it well. The parable of the talents and all that. But really, who knows anything about wineskins? I mean, really! Think of it like a lottery ticket that hit, a much better metaphor. You can squander the winnings or invest them. What will you choose to do?

Her eyes smiled with gratitude. She knew he was right — as he said, she intuitively knew it.

Heidi was a faithful member of The Group, as some called it, or the Gillespie Growth Seminar, as others did, preferring the formal name and not into the whole brevity thing, or "that thing at Dr. G's," as Louise said. It was a learning circle where they grew in personal power, a small floating population that met at his apartment to listen to tapes (discarnate spirits, sages remaining between worlds to help humans climb the ladder), and to Dr. G. expounding upon reality itself, and to play games that taught them to use their gifts. His methods were synthesized from the wisdom of the ages, you tube videos, his own mistakes, and the gurus of the day, mostly ones who made big money on the circuit and lived large in million-dollar condos and sold lots of products. "I am just a vehicle," he said when they praised him too much, his hands folded on his belly, looking down at his slippers. "But I am what I am. I must be, to do what I do. As a result, I have what I have — fellowship, friendship and a mission. Once we understand our calling, we must fulfill it," he turned his own example into a teachable moment, looking into their faces and moving slowly from one to another. "All cuts of beef in the butcher shop are the best. If you have ears to hear, bingo, you are enlightened — right now!" he snapped his fingers and laughed.

Those Zen master moments often disappointed. Most didn't get it. But hit them with a stick, they'd have you arrested. How times change!

He would never forget, he said, the day he became aware of his vocation (until he forgot others things too, first his keys, then names or faces or why he came downstairs, then more and more until everything went, including awareness of the self sustained by social interaction, his own identity, the former frame of everything.) At the moment, however, that had not happened, and the day of his awakening was still etched in his brain. He was visiting a podiatrist named Herbert Wickler in his home office in a large Victorian house that needed quite a bit of work. Outside the window the leaves of a bass tree blew by in great gusts of wind. It was four in the afternoon, shortly after clocks had been set back. In that moment, he said later, he understood what he needed to do with the rest of his life. Perhaps it was the leaves blowing past the window in the gathering darkness, perhaps he had been ripening for a long time and that was but a trigger. What he knew for sure was, he was sitting there daydreaming about a woman named Kay with his feet in hot water waiting for the doctor to do something about that ugly fungus in his yellowing toenails when he slid into a domain of understanding that existed apparently side-by-side with the everyday. He flickered back and forth between the two, seeing and being, seeing the objects in the room for the play of light they were, then seeing a shadow of himself by his side, his center of awareness wherever he chose to put it like a parallax view of consciousness or self.

Dr. Wickler came into the room and thought Gillespie had a stroke. His lips were whispering, "I see, I see." The podiatrist by sheer luck or grace understood what was happening and ran into the kitchen for a bottle of canola oil from the pantry and raced back to anoint him and say a few words of initiation based on his own idiosyncratic understanding of How The Universe Works, a system he seldom discussed in public, concerned as he rightly was for his reputation and career, and when Gillespie returned from the altered state, thinking of nothing, nothing at all, Wickler said, "you have had a phase change, James. Like ice to water to mist". Gillespie listened and nodded and changed the podiatrist's words into ones that fit his own frame, and after he paid the man for digging out the crud from his nails and clipping them, he gave him one hell of a tip. Then he went into the world to heed the lesson of the Moment of Awakening, the day that changed his life. When he understood... everything.

Wickler had been doodling at his desk in the other room,

wondering why more patients did not come to his comfortable office, thinking of a life he had led in another incarnation. He had lived, he believed, on a water world light years hence and had chosen earth this time to learn lessons left unfinished in those mackerel-crowded seas — there was only so much one could do without fire. The story popped into his mind as if it were a memory, and maybe it was. Then more memories came to exist. When he had a coherent narrative, he told the story of his former existence to his wife Cleo, after they were married, an intelligent decision (waiting, not telling), but Cleo was dubious, lacking a similar system of beliefs. She seldom watched cable and knew nothing of cryptozoology, for example. Nor did she know of the Nazca lines. Nor that the Sumerians were taught by people from the sky nor that Africans knew about Sirius B when they couldn't possibly.

She tried to lighten him up by saying, Oh? You channel a dolphin? and he looked at her for a long while before he said, I think you miss the point, Cleo. I do not channel a dolphin. I remember another life.

I see, she said and rose to go to the kitchen, meaning "I see" at a lower level than Gillespie meant when he whispered "I see" again and again. Herbert, would you like a cup of tea?

I guess so, he said with sadness, feeling alone and misunderstood, wishing she could just plain get it.

He lay looking at the ceiling of the bedroom and heard her making tea. There was little point, he knew, in discussing what one does not want to know and the other knows beyond all doubt. He had lived in those emerald seas, that he knew. He was not a dolphin either, he had been a diaphanous water-form indeterminate in anatomical structure. His gelatinous organs, visible through translucent skin, had no names that could be said in English. He remembered gliding through the seas like an immense skate or ray. What species would he have been? He shrugged. What did it matter? What do taxonomies, categories, labels, names, matter at all? They are arbitrary in a world without walls, we use them to make walls, ones we find useful, then live in as if in a real house. If he had not come to a world with land this time, he would have no fire, and if no fire, no civilization as we know it — so, my dear, he explained when she returned with two cups of steaming tea and asked what he had been talking about, really, saying she did want to understand, sitting beside him on the bed and gently taking his dick in her hand, thinking that might help the flow of conversation. But after he tried and failed again to explain what he thought was a life before, he sighed deeply and said, you know, you do not have a clue what I'm talking about, do you?

She shook her head. I don't, she said, but you had trouble, if I recall, understanding my family, too, when we met.

Oh Christ, he said. You mean the Jehovah's Witness thing.

Yes, she said. You were angry because they wouldn't celebrate anything.

He was torn between his anger, remembering her parents, and the way she was stimulating his dick, having it out through the slit in his flannel pajamas. She squeezed it in a rhythm like the beating of a heart and his focus flowed to his loins.

Drop it, then, shall we? I know what I know. Let's leave it at that.

"I am so bad," she smiled. "Shall I go to the garage, with the feathers and the honey, and wait for you there?" Her eyes twinkled, trying to lighten him the fuck up, and she ran her thumb lightly over the head of his dick, which got his attention.

"I am trying to be serious," Wickler said, twitching. "The

memories of your own former lives would be accessible if you opened your inside eyes."

"Is that like using an indoor voice?"

He started to reply but she did that thing he liked and shut him down.

"And these sea-beings you remember? Now they come in another form to teach you how to climb the ladder of life?"

"Don't... stop... doing that," he said. Then, "yes, the pod leader is a discarnate trans-dimensional being now named Alaracon. I think. Alaracon lives on the seventh level and chooses to manifest on ours, which looks to him or her like a patch of white light through a haze, to help us along." It was hard to stay focused, feeling what she was doing then with the tip of her tongue. "Alaracon's words were written in what I admit is a barely decipherable scrawl that I found that day on scraps of papers blowing down the alley. I was meant to read those words and link them to my memories, I am almost certain. I translated the pages as Joseph Smith translated plates, as best I could, although I had no magic twanger. The English that resulted from my efforts is much better than his strange King James. Alaracon's teachings contain insights into ancient races, ghost towns on Mars, and a raft of other esoteric teachings."

"Um-hm," she said, finding it hard to speak with her mouth full. She let him go and wave in the wind a minute, telling him, "Herbert, please don't talk about this with anyone else, OK?"

"Yes yes. Now, please..."

Wickler told all this to Gillespie when they met later for lunch, eating half-pound burgers loaded with onion strings and sauce, sharing an order of rosemary fries at a nearby tavern that also served a good craft beer. Gillespie paid little attention to the narrative that made perfect sense to the podiatrist, shaping the frame of his world, in fact. Beliefs were fine, Gillespie thought, so long as one did not believe in them too much. He recast his experience in his own frame in a way that made sense at his stage of life. He needed a mission in retirement, "semi-retirement, thank you," he always said, and decided on the basis of that singular experience that teaching, counseling, sometimes hanging around like Yoda, waiting for Lukes to fall from the sky, must be it. He hadn't much else to do, anyway, his resume having been rejected by a hundred organizations in scant need of older gentlemen, however experienced, disciplined and wise.

Gillespie met Louise when he went to the kiosk in the bus station to buy M&M peanut candy which was on sale, seeing the sign and pictures of the multi-colored morsels in the window as he passed — a coincidence? not! — and told her about his experience since there were no other customers and conversation passed the time. He wanted to ask if all that metal in her face was painful but thought better of it. She asked if he taught people out of his overflow of experience, feeling the need herself, these days, to learn and grow in a spiritual sort of way. He said yes, I do, in my apartment, Thursday nights at seven. Bring a friend!

Saying it out loud like that meant he had to be there and give it a shot. She came and did bring a friend, a few weeks later, her booth-buddy Heidi, and they both became regulars. Heidi was nearing the end of her apprenticeship at Open Sky Massage, which was expanding into the Open Sky Day Spa to fit the vibe of the newly gentrified neighborhood, and thought she might learn things from Dr. G. that would enhance her practice and her life. Her clients, getting a discount because her certification was in the works, were the ones who taught her what to do, through feedback, Heidi paying close attention to what worked, what really worked in that room, but reflection with a wise elder as well was a good idea — her clients on crisp clean sheets in a fragrant room in simulated dusk, hearing the music of pan pipes as her hands moved in and out of streams of ki that eddied and swirled so palpably she swore she could see it sometimes, but without a point of reference, a philosophy, a frame, for the mysteries she sensed just out of reach.

Her clients were not just bodies, knees over bolsters, heads into head-cups, getting a good deal from a student masseuse, they were mysteries to be explored, origami-like folds of spiritual planes, magical castles like the ones in goldfish bowls that opened into fantastic colorful structures. Her fingertips followed currents of ki into the heart of the mystery, fed by her hunger for knowing and growing and making a little money on the side.

She discovered fields of energy created by adjacency like bubbles in foam. She learned to touch lightly, thanks to Doreen Czerinski who gave her reiki training after class on Wednesdays for free. "Honey, you do have a gift," Doreen said. Hell, the first time she tried, Heidi pulled in ki like a fish on a line, her hands hovering over a prone Doreen on a sheet, energy leaping the gaps. Doreen sat up afterward and said, "Babe, you're a regular little Tesla" (thinking of the legend, not the man). "It's real then! Heidi said. I thought I could feel it! Wow. Jeez!" And she plunged into letting it all happen, eager to be fluent in the language of the flesh.

Dear reader, picture a guy naked on the table on his belly, trying to stifle a woody as Heidi, her eyes closed, stood beside him, breathing deeply to center herself, settling in the rocking chair of her soul, her palms fluttering like birds over his back, searching for a branch, the energy between them already rising as she reached him on multiple levels, finding her way.

A client might say later, that was great; or wow, that felt really nice, or more rarely, what was that, when your hands weren't touching? I swear I could feel something. That often followed times when fields spiked and ki became sporadic, hard to track, making her practically dance around the table trying to keep up, her palms becoming so hot she had to blow on them — whoosh! - to cool them down.

Then she would pull up the sheet and lean close and whisper, thank you, [whoever], as Doreen taught her, warning them, be careful now, when you get up, the client saying, "thanks," Heidi squeezing a foot beneath the sheet a final time as she left, the colorful curtains on jangling brass rings chiming behind her.

She wondered the night of the day they met if Jack felt her energy through her thick mittens and his gloves as they walked in the cold twilight. Layers might prevent an exchange. She glanced sideways to see if she could tell but Teufel looked tired. Riding buses day and night could do that to a guy. He was already weary when the coach pulled in among a dozen others and the driver killed the engine at last. Once he was on the walk, the cold air stinging his cheeks, the earth beneath his feet, his bag on his back, and once he was coming up the stairs into the waiting hall, globes of light appearing step by step as he ascended, then the fronts of shops and carts and kiosks and people, once he knew he had arrived, he felt a lot better.

The waiting hall had soft auras around the lights as if he was emerging from a chlorinated pool. The odors from a dozen food stands clashed. Carts sold scarves, wool accessories from Peru, cinnamon rolls, all kinds of useless shit he was learning Americans like to buy, keep for a while, then sell. They took their cues from cable, product placements, celebrity endorsements, what was in or out. It was new to him then. He blinked as the scene came into focus, travelers on benches or wandering around like lost children, waiting for someone to tell them what to do — which someone did, making announcements that sounded like muffle muffle murghl, an oracular voice posing a riddle, making them work to hear what platform, destination, or time a bus would arrive or leave.

He stopped at the top of the stairs. The corners of his duffle dug into his back and he shifted into an easier lean. Then he scanned the brave new world of an upper Midwest city on the earth.

This was the earth! This was the upper Midwest! This was the city! This was the stage! Enter from left, now!

Then someone ruined it, as humans will.

"Excuse me," she said.

Oh Christ, he thought. Here we go, another human telling him what to do. He knew what she would look like, and sure enough, he turned and there was an obese woman in a purple cloth coat, her eyes a mute rebuke as she went around his hump-like duffle. He watched her sway off toward the doors as if she were a queen. He stared at her slowness, he could not believe how slowly the immense woman was walking. He thought of a mastodon making its way through a swamp. He thought of a some-thing-saurus sinking in mud with each socketed step. She was really slow. And huge. People went around her or got stuck behind, degrading their pace so much they must want to scream. For a lark, Teufel followed her and tried to sync his walk to her wobble. He felt as if he were lifting one slow heavy foot at a time from oozing muck, putting it down when she did, creeping at a slothful pace. If her walk were a voice, he thought, it would sound as if the battery had died, going lower, slower, until it stopped.

He shook his head with disgust — getting into his role, playing a disgruntled human smarter than the rest. Practicing his attitude. Stanislavsky, his king.

She exited into the bright daylight, taking time at the door, making people wait more, then disappeared onto the street.

(That episode was replayed sixteen billion times across the Skein.).

He stood for a long while, looking for benchmarks for what a native might think was real. Their environments were thought forms plugged into one another like a child's plastic beads. To play the game, he had to learn to use their beliefs, waking dreams, vague consensual mental states, to understand how they fused a shared perspective with a "sense of self" which dangled from it like a hanging chad and which they thought all others had.

He looked at a kiosk across the hall, attracted by magazines hanging on clips, newspapers, cigarettes in stacks. A dishwater blonde in a turquoise blouse was behind the counter, her elbows resting on the glass. Her nails, he noticed as he approached, were white with tiny pink decals, pink petals pasted onto half moons. Her nails weren't long, just garish. He didn't see a wedding band, but she wore lots of large silver and turquoise rings, matching a chunky necklace around a throat that betrayed her real age. Tasteless, he thought, would be a step up. She probably bought that crap at a street fair or from some Navajo on a two-lane road.

As he came to the counter, she smiled and stood straighter. She looked into his eyes and his intensity made her take a step back. She felt it behind her eyes like the pressure of a headache.

"You look tired," he said. "Has it been a long day?"

"Jeez, do I?" she said. "I wonder why."

Teufel laughed. "You know what? You're the first person I've spoken to in this city. The very first. So please, carry on. OK? OK?"

She noticed the precision with which he spoke, enunciating clearly. Wherever he came from, it wasn't here. She disbelieved his easy attempt at charm, but at this hour of the day, in the midst of a sluggish mid-morning, needing more coffee or sugar, his charm however insincere trumped genuine indifference.

"I've heard that before."

His smile never quit. He looked at her hair, a dirty blonde that worked in a cheap sort of way. Too much eyeliner, too much blush. Her scent, although it had faded since that morning, was still strong. He sniffed audibly and relished the burn it made in his brain.

She needed a teacher, he thought. Inside his head, she requested a volunteer and he raised his hand. Yes, she would point. You. Jack T. Teach me, please.

"My name's Jack Teufel," he said, reaching to shake her hand. She let him shake it, not giving him much to grip. "I always tell the truth. That's something you should know. I just arrived from I think it was Utah. One of those square states, anyway. I have spent too many days on the bus. Too many nights in cheap motels. My journey has been quite tedious. Not as noirish as I hoped, just boring. I don't know a single soul in this city. How about letting me know... you? Then I will know one person and not feel so lonely. That will help me over the hump. Perhaps we can have a drink? Or a cup of coffee?"

Heidi laughed. "That's fast, Jack Teufel. No prelims, huh?

Straight to the main event?"

"Look," he said, still smiling, thinking of the black president, always saying look, setting everybody straight. "Look, I'm tired too. I've been on a bus for days. I listened to morons and idiots until I wanted to scream. But I had to stay the course, to get here. This is the first act. Or the second scene of the first act, I'm not sure. I have rented a place on craigslist and I now must find it and hope it is OK. You know how they alter photos. A photo is worth a thousand lies. Everybody knows that, but humans believe what they think they see. So I hope what I saw online is what is there. I have to go to a bank to get a key from some guy who works for some other guy, then find my place. It's cold out there, very cold, and I am not used to such cold. I need a human being, a warm human being such as your attractive self, as an anchor, a holdfast, I don't know what to call it, I need someone I know I know. I need to know I know another human being. I have selected you."

Heidi laughed, thinking of Max on *Parenthood*.

"I'm here Monday through Thursday, eleven to four-thirty." She pointed above her head to a sign, *New World Media*. "There's your anchor. Come around whenever you like."

She did not get his drift.

"How about a martini? Something red and sweet with a fake sophisticated name. Or a chocolate espresso drink? or maybe deep fried high-fat highly caloric more-than-salty munchies? Today, I mean. When you get off. Four-thirty like you said."

She looked at his persistent smile. Then she shrugged. Trusting her intuition, just like that. "What the hell. OK. Come back at four-thirty. I'll have a little time. Sure, we can get a drink."

"Hooray! Thank you. Thank you so much. What is your name?"

"Heidi," she said.

He waited. But that was it.

"OK," he said. "Heidi. I am Jack Teufel. I'll be back at four-thirty and we'll have a drink."

She turned to sell a Wall Street Journal to a middle-aged man in a bulky gray overcoat and when she turned back he was gone, through the crowd, through the heavy doors and out into the bright cold daylight.

CHAPTER 4
Harry and Sally
Go to the Pink Martini

"**I** do like that hat!" Heidi said again — not knowing what else to say, but thinking she ought to say something, the two of them walking in silence through the holiday crowd. "It takes balls to wear a hat like that. I like that in a man."

Teufel paused before responding. He didn't know why it required balls. Idioms were non-trivial challenges. He grinned and nodded. "Yes it does. And if I have anything, I have balls." He grinned. "What else do you like? Ugly, lazy, horny? I got them all."

She thought of responding, "You don't look lazy," but held her tongue.

The sidewalk was crowded, the sky to the west a glowing rosy dusk behind buildings in silhouette like charcoal drawings — the skyline a simulation refreshing itself with pixels winking in and winking out so fast that humans thought it was always on.

The starless cloudy sky was low, reflecting city light. A fog of exhaustion steeped in his heart like mist on a swamp. He felt hollow, and the city in which he walked, a longed-for destination for so long, felt as if held at arms length. He tried to feel longing, normal human longing, sadness, nostalgia, perhaps, and the loneliness that humans seemed to have — a state which, deconstructed Harry-like, might mean they weren't lonely at all. Or were lonely together, the best they could get.

He thought of the Skein, a dimmer and dimmer memory, now a few threads in a tapestry of waking dreams. The Skein had emerged from thousands of species (so they thought, so they called themselves, before the merge, mistaking taxonomy for ontology). Every encounter was a trigger to restructure, change names, reset calendars and clocks until they didn't use either anymore. On earth, humans sift through digs and draw timelines in search of clues to origins and draw timelines; the Skein peers into a nebulous fog at the back of its brain where millions of identities are scattered like bones, twisted and spliced by time, by evolution self-directed by the Skein, until time itself, malleable and elastic, was seen to be the only mold. Then time became the tool, the only tool, a tool they learned to fold until times touched, and linking links to loops became the task.

Teufel felt fluttery, disconnected, as if he were outside in the cold wind, which he was, looking through a window, which he was not, his nose on the glass, watching others chatter before dinner. He felt like Dan Ellsberg, stripped of his clearances, standing on a Georgetown porch, his former colleagues mingling in a well-lighted living-room until they turned their backs and went to dine.

Teufel countered the pressure of the human community

around him by exaggerating a contrary persona, seeking refuge in the comic. But he didn't feel funny, not at all; he felt like the guy in *Nighthawks*, aware of his isolation even more because of the couple at the counter.

At that moment, when he was thinking how gloomy earth could be, Heidi bumped him, jostled by the crowd. She took hold of his arm, steadying herself, and smiled a thank you, holding on. He barely noticed her gesture, obsessed with his decision "once upon a time" as stories often began, to leave the Skein and take the role on earth. He was second-guessing his Skein self, which was silly, since a human point of view was inadequate to that. But a human point of view he had, and thoughts tumbled like clothes in a dryer. Anxiety made his pace increase and Heidi had to skip to keep up, thinking, OK if the universe is gregarious, like Dr. G says, does that affect me? — thinking that with one part of her brain while another part focused on the slippery sliding snow beneath the red slick soles of her fashionable black boots, and a third part of her brain, the part that plugged into whichever man was around, paid attention to a now-brooding Teufel. She felt his distress and responded with concern but didn't know him well enough to know what he needed. She wanted to help but didn't know how and skipped back and forth between those states like a needle stuck on a groove. Then Teufel did the job himself, somehow interrupting his obsessive thoughts and telling himself, hey, what the fuck, lighten up. That gave him room to choose and he shifted his attention out into the world. To do that, he had to reach inside as if he were grabbing a charging bull by its horns and twisting it to make it go the other way, reverse the flow of energy, turn it inside out and free himself from himself, forcing himself to look out at the world, and as he did, discover that he could do that for the first time, a nifty tool to have, and in came the roar of traffic and energy in the air and the cold dry night and he tuned in to the woman beside him, putting up with his mood and wondering why.

The wind was punishing. This upper Midwest winter was a demon. The planet was not fun in December when polar air swooped down like that. But then he heard ringing Christmas bells and saw what-must-be-a-woman in a doorway, wearing a braided uniform and shaking a hand bell with vigor. A red bucket beside her extracted money from passing marks. She was not very inviting. Heidi by contrast was inviting — not bad, that is, for a woman her age. He remembered *Elmer Gantry, Leap of Faith, A Face in the Crowd* — so knew how the game was played, an exchange of cash for a "God bless!" It felt like slipping a twenty to a hooker and calling it true love.

He squinted into the darkness descending on the city, as if he had cataracts. The sky was lighter between buildings. The downtown streets were alive with light that seemed to pulse and brighten as he stared, streetlights and windows and headlights uniting in a single grid. His pulse beat to the pulse of the streets. He sang *Downtown* to himself in the part of his brain that never shut up. Her chuckle at his off-key singing made him remember Heidi again, skipping along beside him. He felt her warm presence and let it into his awareness — her game and giving MILF self, how much she liked life and welcomed whatever, a feeling he experienced as a sexual invitation because he had no other point of view. No wonder he had glommed onto her at the station. No wonder her kiosk lit up like a flare. She was an energy source, renewable and fruitful. He could use her to pick himself up again and again. She could give him strength in the sea of broken dreams he felt all around in the lonely crowd, which struggled to oppress him, to mute the comic vibe. Giving in to that would never do, because, he knew, ratings would cave.

He took her hand. She felt his fingers squeeze between hers, sensed his jittery self and efforts to calm himself. She inhaled the scent of his feral presence, the stale dried sweat from days on the bus, an animal challenge that she liked. "You sure like the wild ones," her mother said when she was fifteen, after finding her under the dining room table after dinner where she and one of the boyfriends (Harry? Perry? Barry? Heidi couldn't recall) had slipped for a quickie as her parents did the dishes on the kitchen side of a swinging door. "I guess so," she said, holding the guy so he wouldn't drip on the beige carpet. Her heart pitter-pattered happily (then and now) and she inhaled again, his skunky musk making her want him. Her vagina seconded the notion with a shiver in the chill. She wanted to touch herself but of course did not. For one thing, there were too many layers, she would have had to dig deep inside her slacks, and for another, she had been taught when she was four, no, we do that at home, dear, not in the aisle at the K-Mart. Go to your room — not to be punished, but to practice doing it right, little Heidi assumed, delighted to find a toy she always had with her, rain or shine, before she found the internet and purchased her very first vibrating egg.

That moment of arousal next to Jack was an inflection point for Heidi. She tilted toward having sex with the guy and also toward whatever came. She went all in — but didn't quite know it yet. Still, something shifted. She realized it more fully when he called her late one night, and instead of ignoring the ring tone, listened and responded kindly, patiently, warmly. That was when she realized she had become his go-to girl and went with the plan.

In that moment in the cold, however, she was part of the crowd, their conscious selves like bubbles in the foam, energy and information moving back and forth through porous walls, drawing lazy loops in the brain like swirls on an etch-a-sketch that would include, if they knew the Skein — almost everything, as Dr. Gillespie taught.

The translucent membranes between their psyches, separate fields of energy, allowed feelings in and out. That affected how each arranged the world in here-and-now Heidi or Jack shapes or frames. Rhomboids were tugged into tetrahedrons, reframing previous details in a new Jack-and-Heidi frame — a subtle change, but one with potential. Thoughts drifted like smoke into a cloud of colloidal suspension, experienced by each, by both, as memories — his fingers between hers, squeezing; her warm feelings and generous spirit like a soft kiss on his cheek; their mutual lust, unspoken for the moment; the beauty of the traffic lights turning red to yellow to green, inviting pedestrians to cross — all of it was meaningful, all of it was good.

Heidi closed and opened each eye in turn, getting a parallax view. She had learned the word from a crossword puzzle and asked Gillespie what it meant. He said, yes, parallax, well, parallax is a fine word, it refers to how we see things, now with this eye, now with that, suggesting that a single fixed point of view is impossible. We can't separate what we see from the means by which we see, you see. We use the same words to mean the same things but we don't. We don't mean the same things, I mean. The mind, unaware of itself, creates the ground, then the frame. We see the picture and live in the picture as if. Relationships, you see, between things matter more than things themselves. Yet... entangled entities do seem similar? or the same? — whatever that means! It has all gone the way of 'simultaneous' after relativity, you see." He smiled widely and Heidi smiled as if to say she understood. "Entanglement, let us discuss that another time. It is however the means I believe of non-local consciousness which enables in any case a way to think about how things link.

"But, well, parallax," he concluded, "parallax: in a nutshell, some see right-eyed, some left. A lucky few see both."

He paused, looking into her eyes as if about to confide a secret. Then he whispered:

"I see both."

Heidi thinking, he sounds sometimes like Obi Wan, sometimes like Yoda. Sometimes like an old man trying too hard.

"Do you like *Star Wars*?" she said.

"Yes!" Jack said. "Oh yes. It's pretty close. I watched all six and then a lot of the clone war toons in Enid Oklahoma. I didn't sleep that night. I learned a lot, from the first three, I mean. The rest suck. JarJar? Really! Give me a fucking break."

Teufel was animated now, grinning at a memory of Tatooine, hearing the music swell when Luke knew his destiny. The closest they came, he thought, to listening as he did to the music of the Skein, everyone humming along, unaware of the source.

"Snow dries funny at this temperature. It's the low humidity." Jack said, nodding toward his feet shuffling through the chalky snow. "It freezes into a powder."

Heidi looked at the pointed tips of her black boots parting the snow. "I guess it does."

"It's drier in the average apartment than the Sahara Desert. Did you know that? I heard that on the Weather Channel."

"Nope." She smiled at Jack. "The way you talk reminds me of a guy at our massage school. He's from one of those countries that were Russian. He laughs at things no one thinks are funny. You do that sometimes, too."

He accepted what she said despite its imprecision, nodding to keep the peace. He thought he laughed only at what was funny. But humor is a function of cultural context, which was of course why he came, because humans were the funniest, straight up.

He glanced at Heidi's face in the light. Down at the level of the sidewalk, deep inside the cave of night, she looked like a dancer, a green shadow on her face, a Degas ballerina. The opaqueness of the future was at bay. They might look like Hansel and Gretel, hand in hand, waiting at streetlights, office windows and condo windows all around lighting up as people returned home, buses roaring past, strap-hanging passengers swaying inside, a skating rink across the street where skaters under floodlights circled near a warming house, people in windows looking like grays in a scout craft, hovering.

The city felt like a circus. City life was lived in a ceaseless fall of confetti on a parade of people going to work and going home. "Home," he smiled, was a good word. When they used it, they thought they were licking real meaning like icing from their fingers. It tasted good to say it. Then it vanished, sublimating like the snow in the cold. Because they didn't know, their real home was Foam.

The Skein dreamed of fusion with the Foam at the end of what they still called time. And one fine morning... .

They stopped at a corner for a light, stamping their feet. The busyness of so many people knitted itself into something substantial. He heard the catchy lyrics once again — Downtown! — and his audience felt it. A thrill trilled, relished by billions, saving it for replay. The Skein was into catchy tunes and hooks, it seemed.

Traffic crept forward, going nowhere. Someone bumped into Jack and said, sorry. Teufel nodded, Heidi hooked her arm more tightly inside his crook and flexed her cold toes in her boots, rocking back on her heels. The waiting crowd grew bigger as cars filled the intersection, going nowhere, honking to no purpose.

"Want a cup of coffee?" she said. "Or a drink? I need to eat something, I have a thing I need to be at after six."

"What is the thing?"

"Our group. Gillespie Group. We meet at our teacher's, Dr. Gillespie, he lives a few blocks from here. There's a bar on the way, The Pink Martini. We can stop there."

"Sure," Teufel said. "Whatever you say."

A little green walking man flashed and they hurried among refugees from daylight and work and what they called normal to The Pink Martini. They paused before the window where tiny white lights in dark leaves flashed and pink neon blinked: *Martini's. Martini's.* and bubbles in colors flashed from a tilted simulated bottle to a simulated glass.

She was waiting for something, looking at Teufel, looking at the window, then at Teufel. Oh! he said, pulling out the heavy door like Gregory Peck, Heidi saying thank you as if she couldn't open the door by herself. He followed her upstairs, watching her thighs in dark slacks climb the narrow stairs toward loudening voices and then, at the top, enter the din of a vast dim clamorous bar, the odor of wet wood and liquor, humans in heavy coats, a jumble of talking and laughing: A bartender shaking a shaker, two glasses before him, a middle-aged guy in an overcoat, still cold, apparently, his coat buttoned to the collar, leaning on the counter. Jack watched his lips, heard an occasional word, then became conscious of conversations all around, at tables, sofas, sitting pits, the noise like a swarm of humming bees punctuated with bursts of mirth. Then he heard music, softly at first, louder as he paid attention, rising above the chatter which seemed to diminish as the sound of the music grew.

"Sinatra." he said. "He was one violent son-of-a-bitch. All mobbed up, and he treated women badly, and he punched people in the mouth for no reason. Just because he could. But he had great phrasing. He made people miss everyone they loved. In the wee small hours of the morning. One for the road. He captured well the wistfulness. I myself would fly away, if I could, yes I would."

Heidi raised her eyebrows, tuning him out as she was learning to do, listening for Sinatra's voice. Teufel watched her face as she concentrated hard, doing the thing that Meg Ryan does with her nose, a romcom trope he liked, her features releasing once she heard the signal in the noise.

Her lips mouthing words.

"He is dead, of course. That's only a recording."

"Yep," she said.. "That's how we do it."

"Crosby, you know, was also a cold bastard, distant and indifferent. Is there something about crooners? They sound warm in songs. Perhaps they compensate for what they really are. Are humans often opposite what they seem?"

Heidi smiled. "Some. Are you?"

"Me?" He laughed. "Hell no! I am straight up. People take their Teufel neat."

He watched her watching him, liking what he thought she saw.

"But aren't you sometimes not what you seem?"

Teufel laughed. "Humans are a funny species. You think you

are being specific but you are so vague. Your language is so imprecise. Insectoids have a leg up, so to speak, and I don't mean the other four. I mean the way their buzzing hums. They hit the notes just right."

Heidi wanted to respond but couldn't think of anything to say. Then, "How about over there?" pointing with her face toward a table at the window.

"Fine," he said, letting her lead which she liked. "Are you keeping on your coat?"

"Yes, I'm cold. Thanks!" she said, as he pulled out and pushed in her chair like Tom Hanks did.

Heidi sucked in her stomach, slotting into the tight spot. Teufel looked at the little midriff bulge in her blouse. He saw himself lying on top of her body, licking her belly, nibbling her nipples. He felt them harden between his teeth. His real teeth made a little nibble and he imagined the noises she would make, how she would move, feeling himself harden against her. He knew she would be thrilled to be fucked by him robustly, and he knew how to do it right, learning from late-night cable which he bought with a plastic card. Learning the meaning of loneliness in late-night cheap motels.

He moved down (in his head) to kiss her thatch, wondering was it blonde, then licked her clit, thrusting his tongue in, licking and thrusting, back and forth, gripping her tight cheeks which bucked as he wallowed and swallowed and did it again.

The Skein loved streaming scenes from his mind like that, a kind of sex they left behind. There were eight thousand one hundred forty-seven kinds of "feminine wiles" embedded in the Skein, and those were only what they knew, seeing it in code. They didn't want it back, a kind of communion that felt so body-bound, but Teufel could feel their sighs and promised to deliver more. That made him lick his lips.

Heidi thought he was hungry.

He sank into the seat across, unbuttoning his jacket. Heidi took off her gloves and pressed her fingertips to the glass.

"It's so cold!"

Teufel looked at her hand and its reflection, then pressed his hand to the glass too. Their fingertips made marks. He slid his hand down slowly to cover hers.

"Your hand, too," she said. "It's cold."

She took his hand between hers and rubbed it with vigor. He liked that and gave her the smile.

"What'll it be?"

They looked up. A girl in a leather vest and a cowboy hat, the drawstring tight beneath her chin, her face fake-animated, blank.

"I'll have a chocolate martini. Do you still do those mushroom and eggplant things?"

"Shrooms and blooms. Sure. They're my favorite."

"I'll have that. No onions." She told Jack, "I'll be close to people at the meeting."

"Sir?"

"Something hot," he looked at the menu. The lettering reminded him of droones. "You say that to everyone, yes? Everything on the menu is your favorite."

She laughed. "Everything is."

And the monk was enlightened.

"I understand."

She waited a moment. "Sir? Do you want a few minutes?"

He came back into the bar. "No. I will have… Irish coffee."

"Jameson OK?"

"Whatever."

Heidi noticed that he did not watch the cowgirl's butt as she squeezed between tables but kept his eyes on her. She looked down through the window. Traffic crawled or stalled, more pedestrians fled work, snow banks piled high on the curbs. Thousands of trampling feet made frozen snow slick, people making their way carefully, moving in a thick social glue.

"I love winter," Heidi said. She smiled at the congestion. "It's so… hard-edged. Real."

"Winter is interesting," Jack said. "People go inside, themselves I mean. People in tropics, not. Seeds must die or they will not sprout. Indolence is a kind of haze."

"You read that?"

"I imagine I did or I heard it in a film. I am pretty well tutored."

He was sure of himself, which she liked, regardless of whether he made sense or not. Heidi tended to be what one boss called "agreeable," disinclined to criticize, which Jack felt as acceptance, as men often did, mistaking silence for consent.

The waitress set down a steaming cup of Irish coffee gently onto the table. Teufel smelled the whiskey, saw the viscous skin on the hot black brew. He cupped the warm ceramic in his hands, leaned and sipped before lifting the cup to his lips. Had he been wearing glasses, they would have fogged. The coffee tasted like honey in fire. He licked the rim of the cup or mug, he wasn't sure which, and Heidi watched him with growing pleasure, liking the way he enjoyed that simple act. He seemed so zen-like in a way. Whatever he did, she thought, he did completely. Then she sipped her martini. "Yum," she said. He looked at her lips, pale in the cubist-scattered light, angles of tables and windows skewed, as she popped one breaded mushroom, then another, into her mouth.

He imagined her lips on his dick, her hair in his hands, moving her head to taste.

"What?" she asked, picking up a shift in attention. A mushroom paused on its path from the basket to her lips. He looked at the mushroom until it had the look of a mushroom that was looked at. "Jack? Where'd you go?"

Teufel grinned

" I was thinking about you."

"Well, I'm right here. Stay with me, Jack." The mushroom finished its arc into her mouth.

"I understand," he smiled. "Baby, it's cold outside. You want me to stay."

He watched her eat, licking crumbs from her fingers, taking sips. They chatted matter-of-factly, sitting on different sides of a lot of distortion, thinking the other understood. It was like a game of Battleship, fewer hits than misses.

"Tell me about yourself," he said, and she gave it a try. The noise of the crowd faded. Their words threaded their eagerness to meet cute on a wire like beads. They leaned into each other, activated by the chance encounter as a portal of something more. Conversation ebbed and flowed in the restaurant, in the night, in the city, strings of ki strummed by invisible fingers.

Heidi seemed to say whatever came to mind. Her smile was frequent so he didn't know if she tracked what he said or responded agreeably to everything. He thought she might be like an illiterate using a newspaper as a cover. But then she would say something so to the point that it knocked him back in his seat and he stared in amazement. "You are fucking *smart!*" he said, twice, seeing machinery inside her sort-of-pretty head. Her kind of insight, however, was a puzzle. Her brain functioned, yes, that was clear, but differently. Her thoughts effervesced. They self-organized in a way that was challenging. She might be an ally, Teufel thought, a guide to experience he might overlook.

"Here," she said. She handed him a tissue.

He wiped his nose. "Thank you. Cold air, on membranes, makes water and mucous flow."

"You're welcome."

She was great practice in any case and sitting in The Pink Martini was better than being alone. The rented loft in the Berrigan Warehouse was good enough, but he didn't want to be alone, his first nights in town. He wanted to get into the role. He wanted to be on stage. He wanted to be with humans, trusting his director, trusting the script.

She kept looking down at people on the sidewalk, He thought how, when he nibbled her lip, she might yelp.

"That perfume," he said, "makes me quack like a duck."

Heidi laughed. "Did you make that up?"

"Pretty much," he said. "The words occurred to me when I read them in a book. I found it under my seat on the bus with footprints on the cover. It was written by what you call a 'post World War American Jewish author'. He wrote about a small group of urban intellects in the upper Midwest. I thought I would learn about people here but it didn't help a lot. The people belonged to a very small group and seldom came alive on the page. The book was too thinky. Not enough action, not enough story. He sure thought he was something, though, with his thirty-four inch waist and all, and all those women, neurotic as can be. He did not know, I don't think, he was king of the neurotics. That is probably why he won the prize. Most on that list which I consulted for homework have been forgotten. I looked up winners, using Google. Nobody reads most of them anymore. But they still give awards to this one or that. It sells books. Like best-selling lists, what bullshit people buy, despite knowing better. Like payola, you know? I read that here in the upper Midwest the mob made up the top forty, giving their stable a boost. Do you see how much I know about humans? I see pretty deeply. I mean, have you read Sartre lately? He won once. Do the Swedes who make the choice get a cut? Does anyone read them except people with degrees who talk only to one another about their narrow interests? In Lawrence Kansas I spent two days reading dissertations. Narrower and narrower, the topics they must choose, and no one reads them anyway. Have you read Pearl Buck lately or Sigrid Unset? How about Knut Hamsun? Ever read *them?*"

"No."

"No. They're forgotten, and libraries sweep their books from shelves to make room for shovel-ware, for melodramatic addictive serial adolescent fiction. Entertainment to tame the hump, is what it is. Distract them from reality."

He laughed. "Humans really are a funny species."

Heidi smiled. "Yes, but we're all we've got."

That made him laugh even louder. "That's not even remotely true. You have no idea. But how could you, with your cute little thimble-like brains? How can you hold the ocean in a cup? Heidi, I will tell you something: The Skein spawned consciousness here once upon a time. You can not conceive all we are, including you too, but you don't know it. You are included, everyone is included, but you have not self-transcended very far. You are just thinking, we are one people, here on earth, and a few think, we are all brothers and sisters, mother cow and sister pig and all that. Only a few years ago, you saw the whole earth from the moon. That was new. The day will come when you will see the whole universe, unless you completely fuck yourselves in the ass, which is a distinct possibility. I read a little story, 'Species, Lost in Apple-eating Time', free on the internet. That was a true account. At the right appointed time (he laughed), a species gets it. We are hard-wired to flip and learn. There's nothing to do but be there when it happens. All boats rise on the tide of life. You are like people wearing glasses looking for your glasses. Look for example at those lamps," his gaze moved in a slow circle around the bar, making her look from lamp to lamp, dim fake stained-glass shades. "Electric light is a big deal, right? But it is only one century old. Before that, gas lamps, and before that, it was dark, oh dark."

He leaned forward and took her hand. That interrupted her wondering what the hell he was talking about. Her eyes questioned his words, searched his eyes for a clue, so he looked down and held her hand more tightly. He looked at her rings, the veins on the backs of her hands. He rubbed his thumb gently over the knuckles, making her forget what she was thinking. She forgot she was baffled, the way he cradled her hand.

"It is time," he said, "to tell you some of my story."

"OK," she said. "Go."

"I came here for a change," he said." I lived on the Wasatch Front. I hiked in summer and skied in winter. I went to the funny show in the Temple, I went back a lot until they told me to put up or shut up. Then I wondered as I wandered up and down the avenues. I often skied at Solitude and afterward I sat and sipped a hot rum drink, looking out at the mountains, feeling that deep good tiredness. I often gazed at the golden angel trumpeting atop the spire. The Mormons were interesting, with their fixed grins,

their buzzing hive. I had a relationship with a woman of course"
— I knew it! she thought —" but it ended, as all things do end
under heaven, which is not held to be invalidating," he saw or
maybe hoped. Heidi missed the name of the girl — the important
thing, she thought, is Jack is on the rebound. Good to know.

The breakup, he said, was sad and he felt adrift. There was no
point in staying after that. "So one fine day I boarded the bus,
blew a kiss to happy valley, gave it the finger as many do when
they leave, and headed east".

She asked, did he miss it at all?

"One thing," he said." I miss those scones, they were like
donuts, but much better, I ate them straight from the oven, hot
and dripping with honey and butter. I miss them very much.
There was one place I went for breakfast on a creek. The water
roared in the spring but by the fall, the snow pack was gone and it
spit like an old man's dick." It what? she thought. "The snow line
on the mountains came down," he said, "all through the autumn,
aspen and mountain mahogany, yellow and red, interspersed with
evergreens until one day, the snow blew off the benches into the
valley and everything was white and then it was winter."

When he finished, she had a story, haunted by her own personal ghosts. She filled in blanks and connected dots in tight
loops. That narrative became the context in which Jack lived in
Heidi's mind, inside that doll-house, made by collaboration over
drinks.

"What about you?" he said. "Tell me about yourself."

She tilted her glass to capture the last drop. Then let him hold
her hand again, liking the way he did, needing her a lot, she felt,
maybe more than she needed him. That made her feel safe.

"I do lots of things. That kiosk where we met is a part-time job.

I'm almost done with a course in how to massage at Open Sky. Have you heard of Open Sky Day Spa?"

Jack shook his head.

"It's the best. A certificate of completion from Open Sky means something. Google it. (He wrote it down in his little pad). For me, it's a cross between spiritual work and body work. Massage isn't just physical —"

"I know," he said. (He said "I know" a lot, whether he did or not.)

"I work on the whole person. The client might not even notice. In fact," she looked around for a clock, "where I'm headed next, our group, Dr. Gillespie is our guide. He leads us to liminal worlds and then we go through the portals or not, as we choose. Some prefer the comfort of the living room and never leave. The rest explore boundary waters, the brackish tides where emergents surface. Most of the time, what we seek shows up. Jack, seriously, Dr. Gillespie is good. He knows things."

"Such as what?"

"Let me finish first. Saying what I do. I have a couple of new web sites, I'm trying to make some money on the side. Men, as I am sure you know, are into everything. Whatever stamps you and make you twitch, sticks. Whatever turned you on when you were three. It's imprinting, I guess. People don't choose what they like, they like what they like. I looked for kinks that were easy to film. Compared to people who write to Dan Savage, it's pretty tame. It's cheap to set up, too, these days. I mean, what does it cost to smoke cigarettes?"

He blinked. "Not much?"

"No, not much. I'll give you the URLs — do you smoke?'

"No."

"OK. Too bad. Some want a man. But never mind. Did you notice my boots?"

He leaned over the table and she waggled her crossed foot in its red-soled black boot.

"Some guys love them. Some like what's inside. Anyway, that's what I do, I'll do massage full time if it grows, but I'll stay at the kiosk until I know, and do the sites on the side. But hey, I was thinking, Jack, why not come with me to Gillespie's? You can meet some new people. What have you got to lose?"

He shrugged.

"Maybe that's why we met. Maybe the universe wants you to come."

He gave it a long think. "I have no plans Why not? It might amuse the audience."

Heidi smiled. "Great!" She pushed back her chair, bumping the one behind. The person turned and they both said, "Sorry," which confused him, because how could they both be at fault? Then the person pulled in his chair and Heidi rose and closed her coat.

"I think this was meant to happen, Jack. It was not an accident. I'm feeling really good about this." She waited while he buttoned his yellow-and-black plaid jacket. "Things fall into place."

She insisted on paying, to welcome the newcomer to the city. He thanked her and kissed her cheek. The feel of her soft skin stayed with him for hours. He pulled down the flaps on his hat, making her laugh, showing her he was the kind of guy you could have fun with, but could be serious too.

He followed her down the stairs, let her push out the door, choosing not to demean her personhood by implying she was weak. She hooked his arm and steered him into the wind which lanced into them with its frigid gusts. His forehead hurt, his cheeks stung, his nose ran, his eyes watered. They had to walk north into the wind, then turned from the busy street down a side street and walked past walk-ups, older homes, low-rise apartments, toward a wall of tall towers along the hidden water.

Light reflected from the clouds and diffused through a mist in the stillness of the night. He felt as if he were inside a snow globe, waiting for someone to shake it.

They walked at angles, leaning from the wind. The street was lined with parked cars. Bare branches against the bright overcast, locust trees between the sidewalk and the street. The sidewalks were mostly shoveled but icy patches here and there made them cling and slip and slide, making their way carefully until Heidi turned and climbed steep snow-webbed metal steps to a lighted hallway. Inside were paper slips beside buttons. One was illegible. Another said H. WOLFF AND J. RILEY. A third: Dr. James John Gillespie, Esq. in flowing script.

Her gloved thumb pressed the button twice. They waited, looking at nothing. After a moment, a buzzer buzzed and Heidi grabbed the door, pulling it out. Halfway up, she called loudly, "Hello, Doctor Gillespie! It's Heidi! I brought a friend!"

"Wonderful!" a welcoming voice boomed down the stairs.

They turned and turned again at hairpin bends until they could see a bearded man, leaning over the railing, waiting in front of an open door.

"Hi!" said Heidi, coming around the final turn and letting the doctor embrace her and hold her for a long time. Then, "This is Jack," she said, detaching. "Jack, Dr. James John Gillespie."

His smile was disarming. Teufel understood at once. He countered with a grin like a short sword but the doctor didn't flinch.

Gillespie amplified his warmth, pressing toward Teufel who backed away, then regrouped, smiling as if he were Puck and the other a mere mortal. You have met your match, motherfucker, Jack thought. The guru got it, right away, and guffawed, turning away from the little whippersnapper who dared to challenge his warm gregarious welcome. He bided his time, letting Jack become unsure, looking at the doctor's cheek between his beard and sideburns, blotchy from recent treatment. That distracted him a little — but a little was all the doctor needed: Gillespie struck like a viper, he was inside Teufel's head before the guy knew what he was doing, and before Heidi, watching from the sidelines, could guess what in hell was going on. She blinked as if the scene was out of focus, which it was, in a way, two men standing there smiling oddly with unspoken aggressiveness, so mute, so male. Teufel felt caught between Heidi behind him and the pressure of his host. The guru's energy felt like a punch in the gut, then another, which almost doubled him up. He tried to respond but went blank. The little sage had knocked the stuffing clean out. He could not overcome the power of the more experienced older man. The battle was over. He pushed as hard as he could, but he might as well have tried to push an elephant up those fucking stairs. The sage's strong hand, thick wrist, his muscular forearm (metaphorically speaking, of course) held him back until Teufel gave up, out of breath, and Gillespie, with a grin that signified victory, said, "Come in, please, come in, come in," and Teufel had no choice, thinking, OK, asshole, you took that round but not the bout.

The battle of the Titans over for the moment.

It did not even occur to Heidi who in that regard was more normal that Teufel resented Gillespie's "spiritual" sway over his new squeeze, despite the brevity of their relationship. Touching her, kissing her, fucking her, all in his head, gave him a claim, he felt, as if they had fucked in fact. But hey, it was just beginning, this epic narrative, so who gave a fuck? He felt the pleasure of his audience, the gladness of the Skein, perhaps (he dared to imagine) the abounding joy of the Foam itself, watching from a ringside seat. He was on the field of play, that's what mattered, Heidi was doing the wave in the stands, standing and sitting and standing and sitting, rooting for both sides, unaware that on the plains of life, on the field of combat, the prize might be her soul, and this might be the main event, this was Fight Club, this was the one the cosmos had been waiting for, with fourteen rounds — or is it eleven? — still to go.

CHAPTER 5
I Want To Be Like Mike

"**N**ame one fucking thing!" said Don Coyote. "One thing besides basketball or fucking all those women, Asians, Hispanics, blacks, whites, he didn't care, he and his buddy both, Magic, the poster boy for AIDS, a poster boy for denial if you ask me, do you notice, Pancho, how the sports show shouters forget to say he fucked ten thousand groupies, getting and spraying AIDS all the fuck over like a wildass tomcat, airbrushing his life like they did with 'what would I do without my tractor'-boy Brett after he took a picture of his dick? You know how he and Chewie hung out in bars downtown, hitting on anything that walked. Ever see that in the so-called 'sports?' Pancho, you and I do that, we go to jail, we're on the sex offender list for the rest of our lives. We're the guys who have to go door to door to tell the neighbors we moved into the neighborhood —"

"That wasn't true, Don. They made that up. They make up a lot of stuff."

"I know, I know, they thought it was funny. They have to please an audience. But that's not the point. Truthiness is not the point. The point, Pancho, is, those guys get a pass! Make money for the media, you get a pass. You think *Sixty Minutes* covers the boss's friends? Fuck, no. It's a circle-jerk, Pancho, dark, corrupt, debased, is what, it's the Borg from another planet. They're woven into a single skein, those fucking hypocritical shits. And journo-asstards who write about technology? That Apple guy had it right, if they could do it, instead of criticize, they would, they'd leave the blinds where they hide all day, smoking weed, snorting coke, waiting for deer, they'd make some real money, and a contribution, as it happens, as we do to the cloud of real knowing. It's like banks laundering cash from drugs, dictators, illegal arms. That's their gravy. They get caught now and again, they pay a fine, it's a cost of doing business. Not one white-collar criminal fuckup at a bank went to jail for one day. Not one! They launder a third of the GDP from fucking Mexico, I mean, and say they never noticed! But if you or me or one of the ninjas pop into some site and liberate the truth, leave a crack so light gets in, and out, I don't care who it is, Julian or Chelsea or one of the anons, what do they call us? Traitors, felons, terrorists. Cyber-fucking-terorists. For using holes they made themselves and leave there to use on everyone. They put our heads on spikes at the city gates so everybody understands. Then lock us the fuck up."

Pancho nodded. He looked small in his huge black leather chair like Lily Tomlin doing Edith Ann or a skinnier version of Gibby the Sit-down King in his lair, his multiple screens alive with data scrolling and tumbling like *The Matrix*, which took a hint from Fyodor so that part, at least, would look good, Pancho listening to his somewhat idealized partner in their lair, nodding and saying from time to time, "you are right Sir," emulating McMahon, king of the sycophants, waiting him out, letting Coyote rant until he had to take a deep breath in some cul du-sac into which he had taken a wrong turn, then do a uiey and come back out, Pancho doing his best to see where the road would lead, which was not easy because Coyote's routes were always orthogonal, following crumbs that only he could see — a habit from hiding his tracks when he attacked - but if anyone could figure it out, Pancho could, his internal GPS working pretty well.

This was not about Magic. Or Jordan, in the end. That he knew.

"So tell me, Pancho, what else did Michael do? Besides be arrogant? How arrogant? More arrogant than Darth Cheney, the man with the twisted mouth and endless fuck-you sneer, spitting contempt for everyone he hated, that lying corrupt secretive power-sucking son of a bitch. Tell me. What did Michael do? He trashed everybody, Pancho. He disrespected women, and his friends, and other players, he disrespected the fans who idolized him. He acted as if basketball was life. Hold on," he saw Pancho's mouth open a bit, "I am getting to my point. But first, what is basketball, Pancho? What is it, really? Return to first principles. Marcus Aurelius. Of each particular thing ask: what is it in itself? What is its nature?"

"Hannibal Lecter said that."

"Yes, but he was quoting. Don't interrupt. What, in that light, is basketball? It is bouncing a ball, Pancho. Period. That's all. Bounce a ball. Throw a ball. Bounce a ball throw a ball. Now that's a skill to celebrate, is it not?"

"It is if you're a one-trick ball-bouncing ball-throwing pony for people who have nothing better to do than pay premium prices to watch you run up and down and bounce a ball and throw a ball. Like NASCAR, you can't spend hours watching that shit unless you're stoned or drunk."

"Right! The officials determine who wins, anyway. Like football, the wheel is crooked. So tell me. Is Michael a nice person? No. Is he a decent human being? Shit, no! A good husband? Please! Does he have any impulse control? Yeah, right, betting thousands how fast a raindrop runs down a window.

"Pancho, the bottom line is, he's an asshole. Everybody knows it. They never have enough, those guys. Whatever they pursue, it's drinking from a dribble glass. The more they get, the more they need. They collect empty symbols instead of real stuff. It's never enough, is it? Guys like that, bankers, brokers, guys in cartels, they have to have it all. A hundred and ten per cent. And when did that happen, saying more than a hundred per cent? I give a hundred and fifty per cent. Assclowns. Fucktards! They make language meaningless. How's the weather? 'Awesome!' How's the cappuccino? 'Awesome!' How is it, dying of cancer? 'Awesome!' The language has been debased. Reality shows teach idiots to be even more moronic than they were. Pawn shops, duck hunters, honey boo boo, each is dumber than the last. Cable has degraded the mind of society, Pancho. It's idiocracy time. It goes everywhere, like Deep Throat said — the one in in the movie I mean. And the net's no better. I mean, Club Love. Seth put a camera on a condom but it got pretty boring, didn't it? Hello, uterine wall. Habituation set in. Like watching a grown man bounce a ball, run up and down, throw a ball, sometimes throw it into a ring."

He paused, picked his nose, and with a flick contributed a little mass to their living space.

"Speaking of Italians —"

"Don, what — ?"

"What do they call that other bunch, the Camorra? The ones who're worse than the Mafia. Or Russians. Who by the way own the state of Israel. Ten per cent of ten per cent. Remember that hacker, Gal? He made that program for finding fraud, because they give money to any Jew who comes 'home,' so of course the Russians were all over the scheme, he releases a beta version, he thinks, for comments by the govvies he hopes will buy, and one night there's a knock on the door, OK, Gal is a stoner, he's coding, doing his thing, smoking a little weed, maybe there's a warm breeze off the sea blowing the curtains, the scents of lemons and oranges and hashish, so Gal thinks nothing of a late night knock, it might be a pizza he doesn't remember ordering, so he goes to the door and two huge Russians are standing there. They don't say a thing at first, then the bigger one says, we don't like your program. Gal waits for an explanation, but that's it. Like Pauli, they don't have to say much. They look at him with eyes blank and piteous as the sun. Program? he says. Say what? The smaller one says, say what again motherfucker. I dare you. The bigger one, though, waits, then says again, we don't like your program. So much for hactivism, huh? So much for the Hacker Ethos! Yes, I agree! Gal says. I don't like that program. What was I thinking? I must destroy all copies. Yes, says the shorter one. Right now. Gal is nodding like a bobblehead, pissing his pants. Right! Right now! The bigger one says, we see that program, we cut off your Johnson.

"Yes Sir! Gal says and salutes. And he did what he could to eradicate the betas as best he can and make sure no one paid him anything. Jesus, Pancho! You think Ari ben Canaan lives? Let my people go? Right, so we can use Pollard to fuck you in the ass. Then trade your shit to whoever we like. There are no friends in the trenches, Pancho. Only buyers and sellers. No friends, no allies. Only targets. Remember who said that?"

"Yes. A director of SIGINT, I believe."

"Correct. But no one wants to know that. "I don't want to know!" How many times have we heard that? We follow the money, connect the dots, like Deep Throat said, the Mark Twain one, not Mark Felt. Read Manning's cables. They sure disappeared in a hurry, didn't they?"

"I got it, Don. Please. Come to the point."

"Paperclip. Our Nazis are good Nazis. OSS => CIA was mobbed up from the start. Drugs, gambling, sex, everything. Running whores on the coasts, people jumping out of windows. Cowboys shooting up the saloon and yahooing out of town. But you have to read fiction to find out. Fiction is the way to tell the truth these days."

"You think they're worse than the Uzbeks, Don?"

It took the Coyote a moment to realize that someone else had spoken, so accustomed were they both to the sound of the Don's voice alone. He looked around as if surprised to find Pancho there.

They were taking a break from exploring exploits in programs everybody used (RealVideo, Adobe pdfs, javascript, pick one), giving themselves root. It was less of a rush to find a new zero day, there were so many, and they had been taking candy from clueless losers for so long, there wasn't much of a rush anymore. They shook their heads at the innocents who went online, laughed at what humans do behind what they still call walls. They had been kicking ass and taking names all night, just for fun, taking a break from the more serious pursuit of riding righteously in the night to take down miscreants, to tell the Truth, Fight for Justice (yeah, right), and when they could, honor "the American Way." Then the Don got all wound up, thinking about Michael.

"The Uzbeks, say what you will, at least they have an ethos. What you see is what you get. They thought it was funny, Dom, that interrogator said, remember? when he told them torture might be a way to get information. They thought it was a sport. Then Dom's partner said, oh yeah? ever work with the Turks? They put down a paper and say, sign it. No crime, no perp? Fuck you, sign it. All those guys, 'friends and allies,' any of them would throw their mothers under the bus. Work with those pricks, you can kiss your ass good-bye."

"I understand. We've seen it a lot. They leave you out in the cold, a shit-eating grin on your face."

"You become what you fight, Pancho, that's the danger, unless you're careful. Unless you're true to the code, as I am."

They both thought about it for a moment.

"That's why hacking means freedom, Pancho, like Perry Barlow said. God bless Barlow! He understood."

"Don't forget Stallman. Like John Henry taking on the machine. He almost won, too."

"Yes! Stallman is a jedi. Barlow was a visionary like Lippmann. Stallman is practical like Bernays. Stallman once beat Woz declaiming hex at a party, stoned as he was, code just flowed like quicksilver from his tongue. Both those guys rule. They know what hacking is, that it's epic, it's a window onto everything, and it's how we redeem this sinkhole of a society from its lies, force it to its knees, make it confess and atone and walk tall like a real man. Pancho, the Fourth Estate is owned. We are the Fifth Estate, our mission given implicitly by the way they put power into our hands. We are nodes of power, now, in a net they can't control."

The Don grew misty-eyed.

"Think of the net as a nebula, information flowing, lighting up as it does. It's like the background noise of the universe. But it must become incarnate! It must become flesh, and how else can it do that, except through real hackers! We must manifest the implications of the frame. Forget that wine skin shit, no one knows what the fuck you mean. Writing code for machines that can handle it, more like that, You can't do massive multi-player gaming with XTs, Pancho. A much better metaphor, right?"

"Be like a digital Jesus, huh?"

Coyote considered. "In a way... I am not big on organized religion, as you know, except wiccan, which works pretty much. Remember when we cast spells on the roof of the Alexis Park and turned the tide of the con? There had been such a bad vibe the year before, but the con got righteous again, after we did that shit. Good old Nomad. Those were the fucking days."

Pancho thought he saw an opening and gave it his best shot.

"I understand what you're saying, Don. But... I see things a little differently."

Coyote did a double-take.

"Bull-shit you do."

"Don, you're Barlow's last disciple. The rest have all grown up. Kids today don't even know his name. Everyone's assimilated. The Borg won."

"Oh, Pancho, my beloved squire! Et tu, Pan-cho? Look, dude, I know why you say that, we're in a panspectron now, not a panopticon. See, I can use big words, too. One click assembles everything. Julian did not crush the bastards, I know that. He's in the embassy, they're in Mayfair restaurants having a fine time. See it that way, yes, you might say, he failed."

"Of course he failed, Don. He's like Holden Caulfield trying to erase all the 'fuck yous.'"

"That's how it looks, I understand, to normal human beings. In the short run. But we are not normals, Pancho. We're like gods who came down from the sky. And this is not a sprint for us, it's an ultra-fucking-marathon. I am I, Don Coyote, the scourge of malfeasance, the enemy of indifference. Corporate asstards quake at my name. Even the Feds quiver when I ride down these mean cyberstreets, down which a man must go who is neither tarnished nor afraid. In the long run, Pancho, if we don't do the right things, they win. We know what we are up against. They lie, they destroy reputations, they frame people, they kill. Their malevolence is the warp and woof of the web they weave. Uzbeks? What about the pedophile protecting pope in his Gucci shoes, lying about all the butt fucking behind Vatican walls, including his own? Does he really think we don't know he's gay? His pals make knock-off gowns the celebs wear at the Oscars. Hollywood, shit, it was mobbed up from the beginning. Jews don't get a pass from me. But that one holy catholic apostolic lying shitass of a church is a conspiracy of criminals, and everybody knows it. But still they genuflect to those fatfaced pricks! And give them money! I don't get it, Pancho. 'The Church?' — my ass. They say that in Utah too, at the start of the nightly news, "Today in 'the Church' as if there's one. Instead of a thousand, each one saying, I'm the One, the Only One, come to me, siren-like, singing like the Phantom. Oh, Pancho —"

"Oh Cisco."

The Don laughed. "OK, don't get me started. Back to reality. Hacking is reality. Getting the truth out is the game. That's hacking, Pancho, seeing the links that link into bigger links and loops, seeing it all, at higher and higher levels, while the normals quit when it shades into mists, while we arrive at the meta-level and behold! the whole. We few, we happy powerful few." He looked into the distance, farseeing like a basenji, as if victory was coming, coming soon, riding a noble steed. "Pancho, if we don't do this... they win."

"Yes. But remember what you said, what they did to Julian, and Chelsea Manning. And of course, using Sabu..."

"Fuck that traitorous bastard. Pancho, you miss the point. At the top level where we engage with the code, a righteous hack in and of itself by its very nature tilts the universe and restores balance. Read Perry Barlow, man! Refresh yourself. Get back to basics. It's all metaphysical, man, and that's where I make my stand. Down here, normals can't know. They see shadows on the wall, they're chained in a cave. But up there in the sunlight, we can see. Barlow saw. Barlow knew. He knew layers link in multiple levels, going up and down like stairs in an Escher etching. Not just six levels like the net, but thousands! It's epic. Everything connects to everything else. Barlow knew they would try to put a fence around it, but we blow holes in their fences, Pancho. We work on behalf of humanity."

Pancho sighed. "Don, you make Jane Roberts' Seth-shit sound like a practical manual. You talk about Barlow — ."

"Yes. Because he spelled it out. Keep your hands off our space! Leave us freedom! Get the fuck out! We neither recognize nor honor your laws. We're Lando fucking Calrissian in a Sky City, a Cloud City, whatever it was."

Pancho shook his head. "It's wires and chips, Don, signal and noise. It's transmissions. Its data, man, and meta-data. It's locks and keys, and we know how to use a few, is what it is. We couldn't do it if they hadn't built like they did., back doors everywhere. We don't make them, we find them. They put them there, Don, for a reason."

"That's how It looks, Pancho, networks look that way to untrained eyes, but go higher, man. It's all Idea, a framework of the mind. We're talking artifacts, Pancho, cognitive artifacts, the net is one big artifact. I'm talking forms of forms, man. Once you see that, everything becomes clear."

"Don, it's switches, silicon and plastic, gates open and close, it's logic. If this then that."

The Don smiled, "You do know that what you're saying is complete bullshit. Right? You're just fucking with me, right?"

Pancho swiveled in his chair. He was so light, the chair glided silently like Frank Poole disappearing into space. Pancho was a little scrawny-assed bastard, wearing a too-big black t-shirt, his shiny black hair held fast by a red bandanna. But his black eyes were ablaze, and his hands were wicked fast. When he was in the zone, they swiped the screen or typed like a madman, cutting through firewalls with his own tools. Thousands of apps flooded the world daily, everything plugged into everything else, making coastlines with millions of coves, winking in-and-winking-out so fast, no one could count them all. Pancho saw that and went with the flow. He focused on boats, what he needed to get through, not some messianic ocean.

Pancho studied the face of his friend, Don Coyote, the Don he called him, his fingers picking a zit, eyes focused on rain man space, deciding whether to squeeze or not. His crazy straw-colored hair with which he tried to cover bald, a puffy face not nearly as lean as he saw it in his mind's eye, a hacker of hackers, yes, but obsessed with quasi-Utopian ravings in which he was caught up like Rust Cohle in lost Carcosa.

The Don left the zit alone. He swiveled toward Pancho with a grin and punched him in the arm.

Pancho smiled. "I know what you're thinking."

"Yeah? What am I thinking?"

"You're thinking Barlow-like, that you are the tyranny of evil men, the finder of lost children, and all that shit that Jules made up."

Coyote considered. He studied his right foot, crossed over his wide thigh as best it could, and tapped his bare ankle. "Hm. Not bad."

The Don was transparent to his friend. His thoughts played over his face like the shadows of clouds. Pancho knew Coyote had become a little skewed, but boy, he loved the guy. He knew what he had done, taking on The Man. He knew the righteous hacks that littered the streets of cyberspace. They went way the fuck back to when they played with Apples. He'd do damn near anything for him. He knew the Don's adoration of Barlow was misplaced, but Pancho chose to believe not in Barlow but in the Don and his mission. He had nothing else to believe in, after all, and he hoped he could steer him into the clear before he did real damage to himself, not knowing he was doing that to stay in the game himself. That his attachment was his version of Barlow-worship.

"Anyway, your point is... what *is* your point, Don? I mean about Michael. What were you saying?"

The Don sighed. Even his faithful squire could not follow his thinking. He was a software-hardware sort of guy, not a Big Picture thinker. He knew the machinery but missed the Overall. The Overall was the Don's special gift, thought the Don.

Oh, he made money too, working in consultant mode, showing the Little People what to do. See, like this, he would say, his fingers flying on the keyboard, do this then this then this, fingers flashing and screens changing so fast no one knew what the fuck he was doing, much less how to do it. Which worked pretty well because it meant plenty of repeat business.

His daylight clients did not know the Coyote was a noble knight in a city of windmills, there were windmills everywhere, and the Don chose this or that windmill and mounted the night like a steed, tilted his lance, and charged.

Especially on long winter nights when there was little else to do.

Don Coyote and Pancho Sanchez were warm and snug in their rented loft in the Berrigan Warehouse, four floors of condos with exposed bricks and pipes and a stainless steel vibe. It was cold out there, and only the thought of a tasty burger might get them out of their lair. Even then, it was a long shot, it was so fucking cold. The dark night was their harbor, the arctic cold their foe, holding them at bay.

The Berrigan Warehouse, Unit 101 at the end of the hall, that was theirs. Down the hall was a new guy from Utah. Also down the hall was the unit, empty now, used by Rupert Rapell for Carrie Fischetti (108) before she moved to 404. Rapell came by when he could for a visit. They didn't care about that, what mattered to the lads was Carrie's laptop, always on. Seeing her breasts under the great white whale, that was a game they favored.

When they were bored, they read texts and intercepted skypes randomly, for fun, from the Berrigan Warehouse Wi-fi. Despite the tiny lock on the screen, they owned the network and used it to amuse themselves. They liked to see what porn their neighbors liked, what people liked to hide, which was mostly the usual human mess.

The wind died for a moment and the few stars that had become visible between streetlights disappeared behind clouds. The darkness was even bleaker in the alley along the Berrigan, a long alley with a single light far from their windows, illuminating garbage cans, a sofa someone had better tip a garbagemen to take or it'll be there in the spring, a lot of rat-attracting crap. You couldn't see your hand in front of your face, if you went outside, cut the lights from the windows, and held it up. But why would anyone do that? It was cold out there, not a creature stirring, except a mouse, watching the geeks from across the loft, checking them out, then eating crumbs from last week's meat-lover's pizza.

"My point? You ax my point as our African American friends say?"

"Yes, Don, What is your point?"

"My point, Pancho, is, his airness was good at one thing. Just one thing. That's my point. Dribble dribble shoot shoot.

"That's what works. Do one thing and do it well. Do it better than anyone else. Michael bounced balls and threw them into hoops. That was it! The rest is bullshit, posturing, spin. Hyping the man to make money. Get it?"

"I get that Michael despite his flaws was disciplined, single-minded, and obsessive. And I get that it made him rich."

The Don sighed. "Yes. But rich is not the point. Rich is icing on the cake. Doing one thing well is the point. The way we hack. Capice?"

Pancho nodded.

"Pancho, that's why we are the Fifth Estate. Righteous hackers are the only thing between that dark heart of corruption and truth, justice, and yes, the American way."

Pancho looked dubious. So the Don warbled in a falsetto. "Is it possible, the Coyote is right?"

Pancho sighed. "Your little girl voice needs work."

"Fuck it. I am not doing voiceovers for your amusement. I'm telling you how it is. I am making a point: the elite do one thing until they do it good. That's my point. So I wanna be like Mike. I want that kind of focus in my hacking as opposed to - for example — this is an example — that scattered guy who moved in down the hall? The weirdo from out west?" He leaned to the monitor and the screen blinked. Data points crawled down it like ants.

"I love this program. People look like little dots that move around and sometimes touch."

Pancho looked. That was how they looked all right. Then Don clicked a dot which spilled its contents all over the screen. Granular data. Click click. He clicked again, going down, until there was email on the screen, formatted properly.

"Who the hell is this idiot?" Pancho scooted over and drew his legs up lotus like under his scrawny ass. The chair bounced on its spring, then became still.

"Make it bigger."

The Don did. They read it together, trying to understand.

'Heidi, I am making progress. I am often at the Oasis, 'our' coffee shop now, and I am becoming a person of significance, a regular there, and a normal guy. People think. I am taking the advice of a guy at the shop to begin a blog. Passing time on earth is a non-trivial problem, as we discussed, a problem humans solve by making shit up, then forgetting that they did. That's cool, and that's the idea I think behind blogs. Pretending to engage in meaningful conversation gives humans the illusion of a purpose."

"He's weird," Pancho said.

"'What I do is, I hold forth! Is that perfect for me, or what? It is not as odd as it sounds — lots of humans do it. I hear them in the coffee shop all goddamn day. In this culture, humans talk, and they talk as if they know. So this person at the shop said, 'Jack, you are an insight specialist.' And the light went on! And I was enlightened! I am! I thought. All I need is a few people, I realized, to say so. Then if I engage in rancorous debate with a few clueless losers, others come to believe in me. On the net it only takes a few followers to make you feel real. So I tell people things. And get this: they listen! God bless America! Anybody can say anything and someone will buy it, Make it a book, a blog, a feed, a tweet, an action toy, a movie, a game, make it any fucking thing. It keeps the wheels going round.

"So my blog is called TeufelTalk. Bunny thinks it will go viral. There are lots of blogs, but mine is unique. It must be discovered however. I have five regular readers, but they are discriminating, are influencers like Paul Revere who knew on which doors to knock. TeufelTalk will tip. Already a few retweet my wisdom and I have been favorited by three fans.

"One day I may add bots to my feed like ELIZA. That program helps me when I am sad. ELIZA says, how do you feel? I say, sad. Then ELIZA says, sounds to me like you feel sad. I say yes. ELIZA says, I understand. And I feel better.'

Pancho laughed. "He's impaired."

"Ya think? But aren't a lot of bloggers?"

"The average number of readers of a blog is one, the guy who writes it. Who is he emailing?"

"A woman named Heidi. We ought to check his blog. He truly is not cool, is he? Not like Mike when he passed to Kerr. Steve, he said, they will double me. If I get the ball to you, will you swish it? Kerr is so cool, he says yes, I will sink that shot. Bounce

bounce, throw, swish. A moment for the ages."

Don uncrossed his immense leg from where it was sort of perched on the other, not exactly crossed, a physical no-no with thighs that wide, but at a right angle at the knee. "We have options. Let's see who comes to his blog, what antelopes drink at his waterhole."

The Don got up and went to the pantry to fetch a bag of butterscotch delights. He stood behind his friend, eating cookies, hand over hand, until crumbs littered his shirt and were all over the floor. He mumbled through his crunchy munching, sputtering crumbs as he explained, a hand on his friend's shoulder, dropping the empty bag to the floor: "One thing. A singular vision. Plus hard work, of course, persistence is key to success, and doing little else and per my point? Pancho: I wanna be like Mike."

"Dribble dribble shoot shoot."

"Yes. But… . more." He turned Pancho's face toward his own and looked into his sidekick's eyes.

"I am going to tell you something Pancho. The Hacker Code is written in my heart. I am one with the source code, if you will. The code flows through me. I lose myself in the flow. Do you understand?"

Pancho shook his head.

The Don tried a different tack. "We are all instantiations of the Code. The difference is, I know it. That puts my hand on the lever, the source of the source."

"You know that for a fact?"

"From experience, yes. Nothing else makes sense. How else could I do what I do? I am the Code made flesh."

"Quite a lot of flesh, Don."

"Don't be disrespectful. I mediate worlds like a shaman. I had to happen, don't you see? They made the mold and it stamped and shaped guys like us. We are the inevitable emergent properties of a new way of framing."

Pancho made the sign of a "B," making Coyote laugh, at least.

"It's a great way to think, Don. But we make mistakes. And we have to sleep. They don't. They work in shifts, 24/7."

The Don smiled.

"Yes, but they don't know who they are. Once they sink into evil, their identities obscure. While I know who I am.

"One night or I should say very early one morning, in the first days at Alexis Park, I was picking a zit, staring into a mirror, and you know what I saw?"

"I don't want to guess."

"I saw my original face."

Pancho laughed. "Don," he said. "You were on acid. Who knows what you saw."

The Don sighed. "Oh, fuck it, dude," he said, and went to piss. Pancho heard splashing on the toilet, floor and walls then through the open door a loud fart.

He reflected on all that, waiting for the Don. The icy night filled the black window. Pancho saw himself framed, reflected in the pane. All the lights in the world were dimmed, or so it seemed. A car somewhere in the alley turned over again and again and finally quit. He heard a car door slam, a muted curse, footsteps. Then… nothing.

The Don flushed the toilet and came back pushing his shirt into his pants.

Pancho, not as insulated as the Don, shivered in the chill. He hugged himself, his skinny arms going most of the way around. But no matter how hard he hugged, he couldn't hug enough. The chill he felt was deeper than the winter that shackled the city in chains of ice. It was hunker down time in his soul. The hour of the wolf. The Don could laugh as much as he liked, or call out, as he did, looking at the monitor, "Dude! Check this out!" but Pancho was afraid. What if the winter never ended? What if the sun didn't bounce? What if it went lower and lower and disappeared into the illusion of an invisible summer as it sank out of sight?

Ragnarok? Maybe.

Oh Jesus fuck, Pancho thought. Oh fuck me.

Pancho knew too, but knew something else: he knew that, scrawny-assed as he was, he could hug himself all he liked, he might never be warm again. He knew that the Don had to know everything, but he didn't, not quite. He knew the walls were porous and the guys who took down Gary Webb were everywhere. You never heard them coming, not the way it actually happened. You imagined a sudden shot, but they were much more subtle, they took away your reason to live, left the gun in your drawer, and let you do it for them.

Oh Kay. Who's naive now?

He looked sadly at the Coyote, whose vision he hated and loved, laughing as he hacked, wrapped in his vision as in a cocoon, believing in butterflies, bless his heart, believing in Barlow, believing in spring.

CHAPTER 6
Hello! I Am Jack Teufel! Hi!

Jack Teufel here. Hello! (he wrote in his blog). I am coming out. I am saying hello, earth. I am sitting in a coffee shop in the bitter cold and transmitting a message to the cosmos on a laptop.

I received a message asking me to do that. I made a decision to take the message literally, to be reasonably certain I received it and that it is real. That is always a choice, and there is always distortion. The signal is always fuzzy, What is sent is not always what I receive, nor is what I receive always what was sent. Neither Bob nor Alice nor a man in the middle can guarantee or verify. And when I am as eager to receive a message as I was, being bored and beside myself with the tedium of a Midwest winter, it is possible that I created what I believed I received inside myself. When it appears in my mind as a message or a thought, it is hard to tell the difference. So there is that then too on top of it.

Now, this might be hard to read. When you have ranged up and down and all around as we have, galaxies upon galaxies, moving through membranes of multi-dimensional systems, all linking up, and in quiet moments, have heard the silent music of our being, uninterrupted, a pulse, pulse upon pulse, a rhythm with no content but itself — winking in and winking out like synchronized fireflies — it is so hard to say in this script — English /earth-talk, pick one — which many of you render meaningless at the get-go in any case by using words with astonishing imprecision - it is amazing, really, that you understand one another at all — I was saying, like you, ambiguity is as close as I can come to what you call clarity. But ambiguity raises questions. So bear with me for a paragraph or two, OK? Or if you must, skip ahead. But if you do, you will miss the keys to the kingdom.

Jeez, people, I am doing my best.

Can what is received — if meaningful, if in "words" or metaphors like these representations, can it NOT have been sent? Receiving presumes sending, I am saying, which means "sent by an agent," a node in a network, right? Or maybe it came from the network as a whole, the gestalt of the everyone/everything plus one? That "one" is the critical bit. It underlies everything. It is the rock on which your words shatter.

It must be so.

At any rate, we must presume that a message comes from a brain if it is meaningful (else it is not a message, it is noise, and the multiverse can not be half meaningful and half-meaningless, can it? any more than a country can be half slave and half free)? So meaning means a sentient creature, or an AI, or a splice of both – regardless of whether we mean what humans call "individuals" ("cells") or a big networked brain in a cosmic body, a body-brain, the All-in-All, the aggregate, rather than an entity. A message without a point of reference, that is, without a sender, is impossible, a message does not just appear in the window of the magic eight ball of consciousness, does it? There must be a context, there IS a context, which in turn begets other contexts and on and on, all the way down like turtles, and all content must derive from a context. Then — voila! — the context becomes content, and a deeper context springs into being like an egg-cup holding an egg, so which came first? the egg cup or the egg?

That was a joke. Most humans will not get it, but never mind. Carry on, carry on. *(Mother... I killed a man...)*

If there is a sign or symbol, if there is intentional meaning received by a being, i.e. me, it must have been sent, I am saying. And if it was sent, it must have come from a sender, a source, even if the source is myself, my unknown hidden selves or Self, and even if the message is an illusion, a cognitive artifact my brain makes to visualize a source and feel good about itself. A message in the instant it is received implies a sender and generates links, links and loops, and fills the screen of consciousness like an etch-a-sketch until it is black, not because it is empty but because the links and loops are so dense in their manyness, there is no room for light to shine through. It looks like a nebula occluding light from a nursery of baby suns.

In every beginning is an end, In every end is a beginning. It is a snake eating its tail.

Whatever is meant by "it."

So I receive, or believe I receive, messages (which is like having thoughts) with the locked-in folded lobes of my tiny human brain, made to be as much like human brains on earth as we or I (ha!) could make it, the word "tiny" evoking an image of bigger brains, eliciting a point of reference so you hapless lot can realize that there *are* bigger brains in the multiverse, one of which, for example, is my/our former brain, a large brain like you believe the grays possess, that is how you draw them anyway, a big brain I miss dearly and for which I grieve in my loft at the Berrigan Warehouse... I chose to downsize in order to come as a straight man for your manic antics... still, I feel on my cheek a tear from time to time, which is how I know that "being human" is taking...

(Teufel concluded his post at this point and expected feedback, robust discussion, participation by readers. Of course, there was none. So he was disappointed and added this next bit).

OK, most of you grew bored. My counter says no one made it to the end of the post. OK, it is not personal, correct? Maybe a few stayed but failed to comment. Maybe my readers are all lurkers. That's OK — Pat.

My intention was simple. I wanted to begin my "blog" — which feels like a bog — as instructed by the message I heard or thought I heard in the coffee shop. That message said: Jack, a blog gives you something to do. Humans need that while they wait — for Godot or death or whatever.

Use your "real" name, it said, Jack Teufel, and call the blog Teufel Talk. The readership will be yourself for a time. That is the nature of blogs. All those billions and billions of words flow into the river of an imaginary discourse and the rivers flow into the sea and the sea is never full. Because language is recursive, like the Skein.

No, the sea will never be full. As it grows, it creates a reservoir adjacent to itself which holds the current and future shape of the sea, it is a shadow matrix in space-time, the sea of information holds itself I am saying like a mother embracing not a child but her own body with her own arms. It looks like a Picasso. It looks like Pancho hugging himself in his loft. So the sea is a means by which it is contained and self-constrained, it is water and basin, both, picture and frame. It draws itself, then lives inside its frame.

Whatever is meant by "it."

It is difficult to say in 21st century earth English what is real.

In addition, dear reader, I guess I mean me, for the moment, I am talking to myself, I do this to exercise my brain as I learn to use it in this human space-time dimple. I will try ideas which begin as profound insights — or did, in my bigger brain — but are stepped down like an electric current to a level that can be received by you, my fellow sentient creatures, as well as by an audience in many other galaxies, and by my human brain as well, so I can think the unthinkable, I mean, in that stepped-down way.

It is difficult to say how this works, but I discovered a little story, "Species, Lost in Apple-eating Time," which says how it is, as much as a story in twentieth-century English by an insignificant human can. It suggests as well why stories are impossible to write, as is this blog, because they are limited to what the language in which they are written can express. The categories and distinctions of the language filter out every other thing in the multiverse.

<sigh>

I don't mean to digress or demean your species. Self-deception is a rule for all sentient entities. It lets us dance in the sun until the darkness closes in. A matrix of symbols is unable to point to itself, because then it would be beside itself. So every time we think we have nailed down the multiverse, and say what it is, in words or in maths, we discover that it is just fucking with us one more time. ("You fucking with me, kid?" Bad Santa said. The answer from the multiverse apparently is yes. But no wooden pickle, no poignant gift from an "obese white male."

The real map is never the size of what is mapped.

So we live in a cloud of unknowing. We in the Skein may be mature and you may look like fingerling potatoes compared to us who look to ourselves like huge pumpkins, like a pumpkin patch spreading over acres of October earth with many orange fruits connected to one another — still, we greet you warmly as late relations, spawn of the same litter. We are all one litter but humans are the runts.

Hang in there, humans! There will be others, younger and more immature than you. Then you will understand my frustration at trying to communicate with you. It is as if you want to tell a Visigoth about space travel, as you call it, rather than time travel or space-time travel or more accurately multidimensional updown in-and-out transmission, energy-matter information on the fly, or maybe all of that, in the Bulk.

Meanwhile, be playful, puppies. Roll on your backs like tickle-me-humans. You have nothing to lose but your arrogance, thinking you are the apple of your many gods' eyes, the top of the food chain. Let go of your delusions, you silly little cuties. Admit you are clueless in the face of the immensity of the multiverse and even more, the Foam in which the multiverse seems to adhere (who knows? really, who the fuck knows?)… oh you are small, we see you as if through the wrong end of a telescope, and what you do not know is so much bigger than you are. You have not even gone all the way around the block but you think you crossed the street.

Read that story. See what I mean. If it doesn't help, because the lobes and folds of your brain can not transceive ideas very well — go see a football game. Watch a reality show on what some call television. Get drunk. Do what humans do to distract themselves from the inevitability of death and disorganized thinking.

Damn! I did not write what I intended. But I did write a lot, so I had better stop.

Hello out there! I am Jack Teufel, I come from far away, farther than you can imagine, although far and near do not make sense, when you know how to use portals, and I am telling you a few simple truths, adapting to your planet and how your brains frame. That is my assignment, my role, and I will give it my all.

I am alive. I am here... now... so...

Yo! Humans! (Heidi, ho!) And again, hi! I am Jack Teufel, sitting in a coffee shop, sending to your brains my words in distorted form, yes, but through these blurred words, see me please, a person if you will, saying hi, a friendly-like hello.

CHAPTER 7
Training Wheels

Once he was inside Gillespie's apartment, still breathing hard from the skirmish, Teufel noticed that he noticed Heidi's coat, which he hadn't before, as if her appearance was background noise. In the hallway light, she came into focus. She wore a blue parka puffed up with downy filling, zipped to her chin, and a pull-down knitted hat turned up once on her forehead, the hood of the parka pulled down over the hat and drawn around her face. Her face glowed from the cold and her eyes were lively. He couldn't tell the color, but remembered that women cared about such things according to an episode of *Grey's* and he leaned in close but couldn't determine the shade. The default is hazel, some-one joked on a sitcom, so he said, your hazel eyes are beautiful. She drew back from his looming face as if to avoid a lip-lip kiss and he went around to help her with her coat, edging the little guru out of the way and taking back the high ground, taking the coat as it slid from her arms. Feeling her arms slide from the sleeves made him want her right then. The back of her neck, the smell of her hair. Her body, inches from his own. He had to work not to press into her buns from behind, and when a thread in the lining caught on one of her rings, he gently detached it, giving her the smile.

"They're not hazel," Heidi said. "But good try."

"Green," Gillespie said. "They are a very distinctive green, and quite beautiful."

Teufel fumed. OK, this was Gillespie's territory, and he knew the guru, the Big Dog, viewed him as a puppy on its back. Well, fuck you, maharishi, Teufel thought, we will see, we will see. Adrenalin was still pumping from the battle on the stairs, and his testosterone was high. They had tuned it to the level of a young man's, and he couldn't control the flow. He was always ready to swing, always ready for bear. Being trussed up, his legs tied and a cowboy raising his hands in the air, was not his style. He hadn't come so far to be the tool of a Deepak Chopra wannabe who couldn't even afford to live in a building with a doorman, much less an elevator, much less a view from a terrace of Manhattan and the river. Religious salesguys lived large like cardinals at the Vatican, data-mining the latest fads – diets, meditation, yoga, Pilates, tae bo, whatever the market would bear - racing to stay ahead.

The air smelled like candles or a potpourri shop on the second tier of a mall between a shop that sold hats and a shop that sold games. A sweet mist drifted from the living room to the hall. He saw a bedroom off the hall and headed there to have a closer look. Gillespie rushed to close the door, giving him a smile of his own. So Teufel went into the kitchen, checking out yellow walls and white metal cabinets, dirty dishes in the sink, a dated Formica counter, no sign of an island, no back splash with decals of pretty flowers, a soft floor instead of real tile, not one thing that cable shows told humans they had to have, couldn't live without, pumping irrelevant arbitrary images – stainless steel stoves, granite tops, hardwood floors - into their brains. There was a small table where the sage ate, a newspaper open, stained with food. On his way back, Teufel darted into the bathroom, beating the guru to the punch. The building must have been built in the 1920s; there were small black and white tiles and the shower head hung from a swinging arm — no flat rain forest head with multiple settings to soothe the weary. Jesus, he thought, what a chump.

On the sink, a container for false teeth, a wet towel on the door, and unguents, potions, and lotions aligned along a built-in shelf.

Back in the hall, he looked at a dancing god on a table, lifting one bent leg, its arms in a circle, almost touching. He was taken aback by the energy coming from the circle, almost like a smoke ring, feeling it ping. It made an impression. It must be some healing thing. Was this guy really a doctor? No, not in a place like this, a three story walk-up, hidden from the sun behind a line of high-rise apartments.

I don't think so Mister Deckard!

The scent of candles, incense sticks, the aromatic smoke made it hard to breathe. Teufel closed his eyes and breathed through his mouth until he felt better. He looked like a fish gulping air in a dirty tank. Heidi and Gillespie watched the Felix Unger-like routine, the way he cleared his throat, making strange noises. Then smoke made him sneeze.

"God bless you, Sir," Gillespie said.

Teufel nodded, wiping his nose with the back of his hand. The teacher led the pair into a brightly lighted living room. Teufel watched his host tiptoe-like on little cat feet and thought of the host in *The Bobo.*

A table fountain bubbled on a sideboard near a woman with metal in her face, taking a cookie from a plate, no, two, three, Jesus, woman! hiding them in a napkin and putting them in her purse. He felt sadness in the way she ate, taking the next bite before she finished the last. He was interested in driven human beings who went on automatic, their compulsions more than habit.

A heating system exhaled noisily through a vent. There was cat hair everywhere which would make dark slacks look like the legs of a shaggy goat.

"Beware the hair, everywhere," he pointed.

"I have a roller with adhesive at home," Heidi said. "I use it every time."

Teufel wanted to poke holes in the posturing of the sage, beginning with his age. The guy apparently fed himself and came home without help so he was still sort of functional. But he must be aware he was almost done. He must know that whatever he told himself he had done with his life, however he exaggerated his impact and importance, he would take his last breath soon. Humans had a million or so in a lifetime and this guy must have used up most. If he realized how quickly people forgot other people, their faces and names disappearing in memories that became a mist, he would know his life was worth little, somewhere on a scale from "insignificant" to "nothing."

He was pretty old for a human, Teufel thought. He must have noticed that women opened the door for *him*, his address book was full of names he had crossed out, he scrutinized obits, looking for people he knew. He must have noticed that a body in a casket looked like the skin of an insect: desiccated, empty, devoid of spirit, like a paper mache manikin with too much makeup.

He probably sat in coffee shops with nothing else to do, talking of cataract surgery. artificial knees and hips, pacemakers, GERD, the latest medical tests, he and his pals showing each other scars where growths had been cut out.

Teufel felt the pride of life surge through his human body. He decided to rub it in.

"So, Doctor Gillespie, you have advanced degrees I assume, otherwise your title is pretentious, yes?"

The doctor blinked.

"Yes? Yes?" (said Lebowski)

The doctor smiled and sort of nodded.

"Tell me, doctor, if you can, how many people can you name who were alive in the thirteenth century?"

Gillespie gave him a quizzical look. "The thirteenth century? Why do you ask *that*?"

"Humor me," he grinned, thinking of Tyrell. "How many?"

Heidi was in the bedroom laying her coat and hat on the bed, putting the hat into her sleeve, then rejoining the gentleman, hearing only the words: "I thought so," when Gillespie shrugged, "which tells us, does it not, how unimportant humans are in the end? How provincial your views of your selves, your eras, your islands of time and space? You flicker like fireflies for a moment, then vanish."

The little guru held his ground.

"Very poetic, Mister Teufel. And true if you think of humans as nothing but individuals floating mote-or-dust-like in the air. The evidence for the persistence of the self, the social self framed through interactions, is not good, I admit. That self is an egg in an egg cup, as it were. That urn," he nodded toward a vase above the fireplace, "holds the remains of my paternal grandfather, a robust Celt —"

"A dead Celt, you mean."

"Angus is ashes now, yes, scraped from an oven, pieces of broken bone, filling a vase I bought at a K-mart — to the outward glance, that is. But if we see more deeply and truly, if we see real links, link to link, and intersecting loops, we see that at the least, we do contribute energy, intention, purpose, something, to the gestalt, we do have impact, however small. Our role is a walk-on, a cameo, I know, but a role nevertheless that does matter. We are each small, yes, but indispensable to the whole. I believe the universe needs all of us."

"The multiverse, you mean."

"Perhaps. It is speculative, that."

"You are saying, aren't we special, church lady-like." He let it sink in, hoping his bad accent didn't obscure the depth of his insight. "Denial is not just a river, they say."

"Oh? Who is they?"

"All of them. You hear it sooner or later at whatever meeting you attend. But please, do not change the subject. Answer, won't you? How many names do you know from the thirteenth century? Isn't that what you humans think matters? Names like tags on the big toes of cadavers in the morgue, attached to fields of memories fixed in temporary storage in your brains?"

Gillespie looked at the glow of a floor lamp in the corner of the living room, his gaze fixed on the bright light above the glass, his brain tracing. In the moment of silence, they heard water bubbling, a cat scratching in another room, the wind whistling through the shaking windows. Teufel's attention drifted, noting the furniture, a general impression of yellow and red, big pillows with tassels adding to a vague Asian feel.

Was the sage about to admit defeat? Teufel thought he was. But Teufel was wrong.

"Well, the thirteenth century, then, Albertus Magnus and Alexander of Hales, a Franciscan friar and theologian I admire. Alexander Nevsky, the Grand Prince of Novgorod. There were artists, Cimabue the Florentine painter and Giotto di Bondone, Dante of course. Less well known is Dom Guzman who founded the Order of Preachers. Aquinas? No fool! William Wallace, a man made famous by the deranged sadistic anti-Semitic Aussie, you know who I mean. William Marshal lived then, and Anthony of Padua. The Mongol founder of the Golden Horde, Batu Khan. Then too, Béla IV of Hungary rebuilt his nation, did he not? Speaking of Mongols, Genghis Khan lived then, and Kublai Khan, both balanced in the moral order by Francis of Assisi, who inspires us still, don't you think?"

Teufel gave a little nod. "Birds on his arms, folds of robes, talking to animals, a Doctor Doolittle type. But yes, some."

"And the influence of Birger Jarl, who founded Stockholm, certainly matters. It is a small but pleasant city. Bonaventure lived then, and Elisabeth of Hungary. And Frederick II. Oh, and have you read Gertrude the Great?"

Teufel shook his head. "You sound like Leno. Oh and then there's this."

"Seriously, Mister Teufel, read Gertrude. She had quite a vision. Have you read Saadi? Not the weaver, the Persian poet?"

Teufel shook his head again.

"Snorri Sturluson then?"

Teufel shook his head.

"Ramon Llull?"

Teufel stared.

"I see. Well, perhaps you prefer sciences?"

"Yes. I am a rational thinker."

"Then you know that Roger Bacon lived then and Robert Grosseteste. They were worth something, yes? They made contributions, yes?"

"Perhaps. Small ones, maybe."

"Don't forget the Popes, Gregory X and Innocent III and Louis IX of France. And Marco Polo. Do you believe that Marco Polo had no influence on the world?"

Teufel chewed his lip. He looked like Jerry Lundegaard interrogated by the sheriff.

The sage waited.

"Those are stories," Teufel said, "about flesh-and-blood people who were turned into textual constructions. Into cognitive artifacts, objects of desperate mentation, trying to make them stay. The beings are dead. When you say names, you invoke patterns of words, not people. This is not a seance, calling up spirits by saying names."

Gillespie chuckled. "All history is a seance, Mister Teufel, calling up spirits of the past by saying their names. Then they live in the present, don't you see."

"There is only the present," Teufel said. "No past, no future."

Gillespie winked. "Good, Mister Teufel! Now we're getting somewhere."

Heidi looked from one to the other, confused but amused. "I love watching you guys get to know each other."

Gillespie said, "Is the thirteenth century a favorite, Mister Teufel? Is that why it was on your mind?""

The deflated combatant looked away. "Who the fuck knows

why anything is on anyone's mind?"

Gillespie folded his hands on his tummy. "True, Mister Teufel. We remain mysteries even to ourselves, don't we? The closer we approach, the more intense as it were the force field between us, preventing us going that last little inch."

Teufel turned to Heidi who looked with what looked to him like admiration at her teacher.

"I knew you two would have lots to say to each other."

"He deceives himself," Teufel said. "He can see the honey and smell the honey but he will never reach the honey."

Heidi smiled, noncommittal. Gillespie turned his attention to Heidi, an effective strategy, Teufel thought. "You were correct, Heidi. Your intuition, once again."

Teufel studied his opponent. Gillespie's white beard was neatly trimmed with tufts like little stalactites hanging at the edges of the mustache. His granny glasses hid rather than magnified his smiling eyes. His forehead and cheeks were blotched with patches of recently treated keratosis. His head was mostly bald, but he had a few scabs there too, and liver spots, and a horseshoe fringe of white hair like a stuffed panda. He wore baggy maroon pants, a puffy pink shiny shirt, a necklace of charms or amulets, and thick white socks in backless brown leather slippers.

"Come along," said the doctor. "Would either of you like tea?'

The room was ready for a session. Chairs were set in a circle broken by a red and gold sofa next to a large yellow chair — the golden throne from which the high priest would deliver a sermon or discourse. The room was a tapestry of red and gold brocade on the wall behind the sofa, the yellow chair, and across the room between two windows, woodblock prints. In another corner, a Japanese screen with dreamy thin-ink figures. Teufel was seduced by his surroundings, unaware. It felt good to be inside the warm dry apartment. Heidi smelled like minty winter from their walk, her hair a little disheveled; he liked it like that; he could see dark roots but mostly it shone like burnished gold. Remember to tell her, he thought, it's time to dye.

Teufel looked at the woman near the cookies. She did have metal in her face, her nose, her lips and when she spoke, a stud in her tongue. She poured hot water into a flowered cup and looked up as she slid the spout over the edge. "Heidi. I didn't know you were coming tonight. Who's your friend?"

"Louise, Jack. Jack, Louise."

"Would you like some hot tea?" Gillespie said.

They would, they said at the same time, and it wasn't funny but they laughed. A hot drink on a cold night, yes, that would be quite nice. Thank you very much.

Heidi shivered, thinking of temps headed into single digits, a wind chill so low the weather guy wouldn't say, getting hate mail when he did.

Gillespie offered mint, chamomile, apple cantata, strawberry patch, or lemon mischief.

"No rooibos jasmine?" Heidi said.

"I'm afraid not," said the doctor. "I'm sorry. I will get more. Have you tried slippery elm? It's good for nerves."

"And glands," said Louise.

"I'll have peppermint, thanks. That one."

Teufel watched her lower the bag and pour the steaming water. He looked at the bubbling glass bowl, filled with odd rocks. "What is that?"

"Ah," said the doctor. "You are very observant, Mister Teufel. That is a table fountain. I have chosen certain geodes, crystals and agates. Their aromas will support our work. They create a frame for the group mind. Like rituals and rites. Frames are training wheels, you know. They contain us until we don't need them any more. The moment our fathers release us and we ride on our own is exhilarating. Everything I will say, once we begin, will be part of creating such a frame, designed to contain the spirit as it flows. Otherwise we might drift. We must remain hard-edged, crisp. We must remain attentive to our task."

"Speaking of the fountain, where's Pyewacket?" Louise said, sitting in one of the chairs and balancing her tea on her lap, her gray wool slacks pulling tight on her ample thighs.

"Hiding," smiled Gillespie. "She's still skittish. Louise remembers," he told the others, "I designed the fountain for my cat."

"Of course," said Jack, pouring hot water over blackberry sage. "A fountain for a cat makes sense."

"Well?" Louise said. "Didn't it--?"

"Yes! In fact —" The buzzer buzzed and Gillespie left to welcome another. Heidi, on the sofa, patted the puffy cushion. "Sit here, Jack."

Gillespie returned with a tall thin thirtyish guy in a dark blue parka, a gray wool cap pulled down on his forehead, He removed thick gloves and his coat, wearing a baggy navy sweater and cheap jeans. He tossed everything onto a chair in the corner and sat.

"This is Jack Teufel, Heidi's friend," Gillespie said. "Jack, this is Lee."

Lee nodded, not shaking hands. His eyes looked off into rain man space. High on the spectrum, Teufel decided.

Then Mary arrived, older even than Gillespie, a small woman with gray hair, into her seventies, eighties, maybe? She was layered in blacks and maroons against the cold. She shook Jack's hand warmly, and in came Long John Greves, making an entrance, stomping snow from his cowboy boots in the hall before exploding inside with big booming hellos, linking them all to himself. He filled the space, claiming the center, appointing himself the king.

Jack said hello, using the smile Heidi liked.

"Will Jeanine be here?" Louise asked. "I have something I need to give her."

"No," Gillespie said. "She was not feeling well."

"Nothing serious, I hope?"

"A cold, I think."

"Who knows what is wrong with another?"

Louise looked at him, then laughed. "You're a funny guy," she said.

"Funny, yes, and interesting," Gillespie said. "Yes, Heidi? Interesting?"

Heidi was noncommittal.

Once they all had tea or not and were seated, Dr. Gillespie stood in front of the yellow chair, defining himself as the leader. He looked around with a smile and waited until they were still.

"Welcome!" he said. "Welcome to the Circle of the White Light."

Everybody murmured hello, some smiling at one another, Long John reaching across to pat Heidi's hand and hold it a little too long. Teufel between Heidi and Mary, Lee across, next to Louise, his knees together, fingers flexing, fingernails bitten to the quick. He reminded Jack of a Hanson brother without glasses.

"Everyone is aware of our purpose," Gillespie said, "except perhaps Jack, who is here for the first time and is –perhaps? a potential member?" He arched his brows and Teufel shrugged. "Well, time will tell. There are no fees, Jack, the only requirement is a willingness to be open."

"Got it. Right."

"Well — let us stand. Jack, if you have a question, please, ask."

Everybody rose, taking the hands of the ones beside. Heidi held his warmly, her thumb running over the top of his hand, giving him an erection. Mary's hand rested lightly, barely there. It felt like a tissue — a *Kleenex*, he remembered — wafer-thin, with veins he could feel with his thumb.

He saw through half-open slits that others closed their eyes as Gillespie said with a preacher's tone:

"Benevolent Spirits! We invoke the white light of your protection and beseech you to surround us with your love. May Truth be spoken, Truth alone be heard. Align us with your purpose that we may leap from link to link and node to node and loop to loop."

"Like goats," said Jack. "Animals with horns." Giving Greves the look, letting him know he knew.

"We ask this in the name of the One God if there is only one or many gods if there are many or spirits all around if there are and if they don't scale to a single point and integrate into a unified whole."

"Whoever, in other words," said Jack. "I mean, who knows? You covered all the bases. That was pretty good."

Gillespie pumped up the volume.

"Benevolent spirits, open wide the portal…"

"Ahhhh," said Jack, pretending that "open wide" was from the dentist he loved in *Little Shop of Horrors*. Then he turned his head to the left and coughed.

Everyone ignored him, as best they could. Gillespie had paused, letting an ellipsis do a little work, getting them into the mood. Teufel smiled at the silliness and cant, but felt his guard going down in spite of himself. He must be tired, he thought, coming to the end of his first long day in the city. That made him vulnerable. Keep your guard, he thought, the fuck up.

The doctor's delivery amused him, sort of a high church Anglican nasal twang that signified "sacred." He noticed as well that as manipulative as the guru's patter was, it calmed him too. It seemed to calm them all. He tried to maintain a derisive edge but slipped nevertheless into a hopeful mode.

Humans must be hard-wired to respond to that stuff. And the hot tea was a nice touch. The warm apartment was soporific. And he liked how Heidi's thumb never stopped caressing his hand, making his erection tickle his jeans, asking politely, may I please go outside now and play? Heidi would say, metaphorically speaking, is your homework done? Oh yes, he would say. Please? in the way that men do when they need it so much. My testicles are aching. Please?

Gillespie continued to speak, his words background noise to the luminous fog of Teufel's human thinking. His sexual desire meant that attention to his defenses lessened. Gillespie was sneaking in through a back door into his life. He felt the people around him sort of merge, surrender their identities. They were like children regressing in the presence of a father. Inside, they curled into fetal positions, they relinquished their autonomy, they became cells in a single body. The energy in the room flowed and pulsed and glowed as their boundaries dissolved.

"May the white light unite us with the spirits who attend us. May their light shine in our hearts and may we all surrender to their purpose."

The group sank into itself, steeped in silence. They were all content for the moment to wait, hands folded, tucked in, alert.

This is interesting, Teufel thought, watching how he took the bait. He bet it played well as an episode too (he learned later that it did, second only to his first round of sex with Heidi).

"Now," Gillespie said, "if anyone wishes to acknowledge errors in thought or deed which might interfere with their spiritual progress, now is the time."

"Now is always the time," Teufel said.

Louise said, "I am angry at my mother. We had another fight. She was drunk of course, there were bottles in the trash. For the umpteenth time."

Mary said, "I resent my arthritis. I hate it. It is eating my knees."

Lee was silent. Long John blurted six or seven paragraphs of minor lapses, easy to admit but impressing the group with their sheer muchness. He ran them off like a Kerouac draft. Sometimes Gillespie said, "John, you are forgiven" or "That too, you are forgiven" or "yes, that as well,"

Heidi said, "I am irritated with the assclowns who email nasty comments. Always anonymous, of course. They get what they want, but they don't care, they always want more. Or it isn't just right for their fetish. Roni, my favorite model (her only model, she might have said) exhales the wrong way or when her pump finally falls, the polish is the wrong color or they wanted natural nails —"

"It's always more!" Teufel said. "They always want more!"

"You are forgiven, Heidi," Gillespie said. "Remember, dear, young people today are uncivil. It's the internet, you know, cable TV, talk radio, shout shows. (What? Teufel thought vaguely somewhere in his brain. Those are my sources...) They call me assclown as well, when I post deep spiritual truths on my site. It is invincible ignorance, my dear, a slashdot mindset. We must forgive them, if we can, the little pricks."

"They're idiots," Greves said, piling on. "Give me their email, Heidi. I'll hack those bastards back so hard they —"

"Please," Gillespie said. "Anyone else?"

Silence.

He raised his right arm and told evil spirits to leave at once. "Spirits of dissension, anger, rudeness, depart!" Then he modified his tone and thanked angels, space brothers, Native American guides, and other benevolent spirits for guidance and protection. Then he said, as if to seal the deal, as if he could do it with words:

All. <pause> is. <pause> forgiven.

If wishes were fishes, Teufel thought.

Those who knew the drill said, "Yes it is. We accept forgiveness, Spirits of the White Light."

Gillespie cried: "O spirits of the White Light! We invoke your power! Align our vibrations to your frequencies. Synchronize us, please, that we may manifest your inexplicable splendor in Ionian white and gold."

They released hands and sank to their knees. Teufel had no choice but to go along, feeling Mary and Heidi kneeling beside him, Mary making noises, shifting so her knees wouldn't hurt. Kneeling made him feel even more like a child, which was, of course, the point, letting Gillespie stand in for fathers and mentors and spirits who hovered in shadows out of sight.

"Close your eyes, children. Experience the spirits around us, experience yourselves in the All – for you are. We are. We are all in the All."

Through half-closed quivering lids, Teufel saw vague shapes

become like sticks in a bundle, magnifying their strength. He let it happen. Why not? It did in fact feel like training wheels, giving him stability, letting their energies move him along.

"Now look within," Gillespie said. "Look into the darkness. There among the mist, see a glowing coal. Allow the spirits to breathe upon the light, making it brighter. See the coal glow, feel its warmth. Feel its heat. See it catch fire, see flames leap in the darkness until there is only light. Feel the spirits pacify your restless souls and lead them into the light."

He paused to let their imaginations work. The temperature, Teufel thought, did rise in the room. It was much warmer, his forehead was damp and sweat on his back felt like the footsteps of a mouse.

"The fire illuminates an entrance to a cave... see it emerge in the darkness. Then move toward the cavern – slowly! slowly! — and see who awaits.

"OK then! Enter the cave. Who is within?"

He paused.

"See Dick run," Teufel said. "See Spot go into the cave."

" Please! — see who is within... is it a wise man? Or woman? Whoever, they have been waiting." He let them pick one. "He or she has been waiting for you to come to the cave the womb the tomb to be transformed. The readiness is all. Now it is up to you. You must ask in order to receive."

Teufel was rapt, in spite of himself, watching some form emerge in his mind, a little maharishi, thinner than Gillespie but every inch a guru, his ancient face defined by the light of the fire, his eyes... jeez! Looking at him with ferocity at first.

The guru gazed with calm intensity into his eyes, aligning Teufel with his vibe.

"When you are ready… ask. Then listen."

Inside his head, the darkness brightened. His little wise guy sat in a lotus or some Zen thing on bony legs, a skinny guy in a loin cloth, perfectly poised. The loin cloth caught the firelight like folds of cloth in a painting by an old master. He felt the earth under him. He smelled bat guano and sneezed. That got the attention of the guru who tilted his head, his hands upturned on knobby knees, his eyes bright. The wrinkled loincloth crinkled in the firelight. Teufel saw his shadow on the wall of the cave. The adept sat as razor-straight and still as a windless flame. Light transmogrified into an ambient glow that suffused the interior of the cave, the interior of his own mind. Ha! he thought. This is what humans can do. It's a real beginning. isn't it?

Their energies gave him equilibrium, aligned him with their purpose. He was present to his guide waiting in his waking dream. He wasn't even pissed at Gillespie anymore. He wasn't even thinking of fucking Heidi — well, maybe a little. Mostly, though, he was *there*.

The training wheels kept his wobbly psyche steady, locking him in as he gazed at the hermit, whose eyes sparkled with mischief. Then he winked, taking Teufel aback, and spoke in a dark language.

"Jack Teufel," said the sage, "you are so full of shit. Can we get that out of the way? What a persona you've picked! Christ! Look, Teufel's not your real name. We know that. You showed up because you were told to show up, but you don't know, do you, what the fuck you're doing here, really. Do you?"

Teufel stared.

"Speak, dummy! Speak!"

"No," Teufel said inside, thinking, I am talking to myself. No one can hear us — me, I mean. This little prick is mini-me. Me after a century of sitting in a cave listening to nothing. "I'm on a random walk. We have a script but it's very loosely written. If I need direction, they'll provide it. Improv is the deal. My job is to always say yes. If I am unable to transceive, they'll use others here on earth, repeaters, and tweets, and texts. They can use other media. They're better than the NSA. My job is simple: let it happen, and wait for the right moment. In comedy, timing is everything. Waiting is something you should know about, if anybody does. All you do is sit in this fucking cave, isn't it?"

"Fair enough," said the guru. "But we're not here to talk about me, are we?" Teufel shook his head. "Well, you have balls, I admit that. And you know what? You'll need them. But balls are a dime a dozen. I can get you a ball by three o'clock."

Teufel blinked. "What?"

"What's not a country. Say what again motherfucker. I said, I can get you a toe by three."

Teufel screwed up his fake face inside his real head. "What the hell are you talking about?"

The guru thought a bit, then said, "Sorry. The streams crossed. That can happen. But back to my point. I know who you are. So don't fuck with me. You need human resources, right? You're a human, prickhead, like it or not, this is the form of your presence here on earth. You can listen to the music of the stars all you like, you still have to fall back on what humans can do, see what I mean? Well, I'm your source, dipshit. I'm inside, the best you got. I can help you transcend this fucking mess. Do you get that, you arrogant asshole?"

Teufel said nothing.

"There are lots of personas to pick. They're potentials hovering like the grins of Cheshire cats. Is the cat dead or alive? Take a peek! It works like that with personas too. One becomes real when you *do* something. Then the rest disappear. It's pretty simple. Every act has like a cone going back and forth in both directions, all that came before, all that follows. But acts interact with other acts too. No wonder things get so damned complicated, what with one thing leading to another. To humans, it looks like a ball of tangled yarn. To adepts like myself, it has clarity. I see each thread distinctly. You'll want help, you know, when you can't see your own hand in the dark.

"So go ahead, use that Teufel-talking dummy. Take yourself through a maze of twisty passages, transceive to the trans-galactic masses who, you hope, are amused enough to want a second season. But remember, there are a hundred ways you can fuck up, and if you can think of fifty, you're a genius. And you know what, Jack?"

"What?"

"You ain't no genius. Remember who told me that?"

Teufel did.

"OK. So… expect the unexpected — on this plane, not where I live, up here, where everything scales, and I see far while you're stuck in near, down where the bottom-feeders live, inside your primitive body/brains. Things down there look like they just happen to happen. They don't, but you can't see, so you have to take it on faith. Can you? Trust that it will all come together at the end? It will, I think, I'm pretty sure. I hope so, at any rate. Who the fuck knows?

"So? We cool?"

"I guess."

The maharishi sighed. "You are such a horse's ass." He shook his head. "Listen. This is important. You know how to find me. Just come back to this cave. Or allow my emanations to expand upward and outward into your everyday ways. And Jesus, Jack! Please. Grow the fuck up."

Jack wanted to swing at the little prick but had no idea how.

"Oh damn," the guru said. "I'm fading. The energy's diminishing. We haven't even talked about..." his voice was growing smaller.

"What?"

But the hermit disappeared, darkness knitting his vague form into an opaque mass.

He shouted his last words with a great effort:

"The detours, Jack! Remember that! The detours!"

His words dopplering toward a vanishing point. Then the chat in the cave was history, distorted like the rest. Teufel's eyelids flickered, and he came back into the world of his senses, seeing filtered light through his closed lids. Then he felt the floor, aware that his knees hurt, and heard the others shuffling. Louise said "yes I heard what I needed to hear," and Mary said, "yes I heard what I needed to hear," and he guessed it was his turn next so he said, "Me too."

Their laughter shattered the spell. They were jerked out into the bright light of the living room. They were back in their social selves, squinting at flesh-and-blood people in a circle in a room.

"Allow yourselves to reintegrate," Gillespie said. "Be gentle with yourselves. Treat yourselves as if you love yourselves."

"Be gentle," Teufel said, gently.

He *is* cute, Heidi thought, looking at her buddy beside her. Teufel felt her looking and turned. They smiled at one another and Gillespie said, "Let us greet one another in peace."

Everybody getting up, Mary leaning on his arm as she rose stiffly, saying, "oof!" until she was standing. He turned to help Heidi, letting her use his hand. Then they were all standing and hugging. Long John hurried to hug Heidi. Mary turned toward Teufel and gave him a gentle A-frame hug. Louise, next, pressed her studded cheek to his, Lee greeted him quirkily with a jittery double pump, then the group waited as Gillespie embraced each in a long hug, holding them close and purring low in his throat.

When he had apparently had enough, he said, "Wonderful. Wonderful." He backed toward his throne and plopped onto the cushion, his feet coming off the floor.

"Before we continue, shall we take a break?"

"Yes!" Greves said, heading for the bathroom.

It felt like waking after a long hibernation, trying to align with the sensible world. The lights of the living room blared like trumpets.

"Jack?" Heidi said. "You OK?"

"I guess so. I'm tired. That took a lot of energy. I didn't expect. "

"Do you want to stay? There's more."

"No."

Gillespie overheard. "Jack, this part is quite interesting. It's based on psychometry —"

"Not tonight," Teufel said. "I am very tired. I have had a very long journey."

"Of course," Gillespie said. "Another time?"

"Perhaps."

Heidi liked to complete evenings but was loyal to her friends — it made her feel whole. Loyalty simplified everything.

"Let's get our coats."

Jack shook himself like a dog coming out of the water.

"Maybe we should eat," he said.

"There's a coffee shop down the street. They have pastries. Biscottis. Croissants."

"Whatever."

They said good-bye, waving all around. Gillespie led them to the stairs and they galloped down around the hairpin bends and out into the bitter cold, onto the sidewalk, under a starless sky, and hurried toward the coffee shop.

CHAPTER 8
The Indian and the Fortune Teller

Standing at a gas pump in front of a convenience store, his hand on the cold nozzle, Bobby Jakus wondered if he were going crazy. If I am, he thought, it's all right with me.

He was certainly a long way from clarity or balance, a long way from the far shore toward which he might not even be sailing. How could he know, prior to arrival? How could the fragments of a mind know in advance if they would coalesce again, when the mind is the means by which one knows? Because if they don't… so Bobby J navigated by faith through dark waters, shrinking from the cold spray — cold, yes, he knew he was cold, that was an ineluctable fact, calibrated to quantifiable feedback — Bobby lapsed from his internal focus which kept him unaware of the cold and found himself in his body, dancing in the frigid wind in a vain effort to stay warm. He watched the flurry of dollars and gallons and listened to the periodic ring of a bell on the slow pump. The bell, he believed, was an echo of the voice of an angel here in the grosser material world, chiming glad tidings in the bleak midwinter. Ring ring! Ring ring! Every ring was a note of hope: *Hold on, Bobby! You may be more frozen than chosen, but hang on! We're with you!*

Those words were a paraphrase of what had been written through his cramped hand, translating the message through the course circuitry of his body/brain. He wrote in a trance in a shaky ragged script. He got the idea from reading books –old books, the original SPR, Myers, Lodge, Balfour, William James, then Yeats. They taught him how to let go and slip into an altered state like a suicide sliding into the icy waters of the lake. He loved and feared that tainted state, not knowing why. He negotiated a compromise with his crotchety feelings and vowed he would never go there during daylight, he would discipline himself to wait until sundown like a drinker watching the yardarm and the sun. Unaccountably his memories of Alaracon's recent communication set off qualms of anxiety fluttering in his chest. He felt as if his sternum were a wishbone, waiting to be split.

He didn't need spirits to tell him he'd get the short end.

Anxiety swelled in his chest like expanding gas. He felt as if an elevator had suddenly dropped too fast. He needed a distraction. He jittered at the gas pump as far as holding the nozzle would allow, dancing in a semi-circle, covering his disquiet with incongruous behavior.

The spirits had rules, but he couldn't always figure them out. They almost never spoke directly during the day. Maybe it was something about wavelengths or calibrating vibrations between their states. At most they impinged on his thoughts, mostly with impressions, manifesting a sense of presence around the curve as it were of his mind. He could feel them hanging back in the shadows, waiting for the right time. Mostly they encouraged him or — if they articulated words he could hear — gave advice. Watch out for that Ford Taurus! Stay on the curb! Turn at the next corner!

Sometimes they chastened him with stern directives.

He always took their advice. If he had failed to see the Taurus, the voice would say, see? We helped you avoid a disaster. Or if he stayed on the curb and nothing seemed to happen, the voice would say, see? We kept you safe. Or, a word to the wise. Or, a stitch in time.

The clunk of the gas tank coming full shut off the flow. He squirted in a little more, making it even, and went inside and paid with cash. The middle-aged half-bald Indian man, Lakshman Noorkhan, made change instead of conversation. He did not enjoy working at the Stop-n-Go but was happy to have a job. He spent long days and some nights selling gas, candy, pepperoni sticks and doughnuts to people like Bobby Jakus. A radio played behind thick glass plastered with ads for the lottery. Should he buy a ticket? Bobby asked himself and whichever spirit was in the shop. He left coins and three singles in the depression and stood still, listening to faint pop rock, then looking at a cappuccino machine across the store, fixing his attention on an arbitrarily chosen... thing... a material thing... so their guidance, if they chose, could slide into his mind through the back door as it were.

The coffee dispenser took on the look of a cappuccino machine that was looked at. A person without discernment might think he was staring at nothing. Bobby would have replied, not! It was like a crystal ball, a thing on which to focus while boundaries wavered, then went down. Then you had better stay there and not look directly. Then you had better let it happen, that was all. Then you could pick up whatever, but a guy had to be careful, he had learned, thoughts and messages looked the same to the up-top part of the mind. Remote viewers knew that too. Discernment was imperative, and even then, they made plenty mistakes.

Lakshman Noorkhan watched from behind the glass. The young man's behavior was no more bizarre than most. Nobody, nothing said a word. No one wanted him to get rich quick. So he took his money and left and got back into his battered Dodge Dart, waiting before he pulled away.

Again, no one spoke. The air was dead, heavy. His breath fogged the windshield. No marks appeared in the mist. He turned on the ignition, then the heater, and watched the vapor dissipate.

They saved him a ton of money. Twelve times this month he might have bought tickets but no one told him to go ahead. Later Alaracon said his numbers would have lost.

Jakus pulled into traffic and abruptly turned right, heading south, away from home.

Thinking, hmmm. Why did they want me to do *that?*

Sitting upright and relaxing at the same time, Bobby positioned his hand with the pencil in it above a piece of empty paper. He allowed his forearm to rest gently against the table's edge, his palm on the bottom of the page. The tip of the pencil barely touched the paper, not making so much as a whisker.

Closing his eyes, he heard the furnace below blasting hot air, tires churning in snow under his window, Mrs. Mortimer's dog Little Buster barking faintly from above.

The snow was really coming down. A girl must have fallen in a snow bank and gave a shriek. Then she was quiet again. The wind moaned through his leaky wood-frame window and made the shade flap. Twelve candles in wrought-iron stands were placed at precise intervals around the room. Whale songs accompanied by flutes played through muted quadraphonic speakers. Aromatic incense lent its suggestive fragrance to the mix. There was little furniture in the room. His guides had told him a week ago to get rid of the old sofa and he dumped it over the back balcony that night. It was still in the alley, last time he looked, covered with snow. Big pillows were arranged around the room and a nightlight from the bedroom looked on the hardwood floor onto which it spilled from the hallway like the light of the full moon.

He sat at the table, waiting, breathing deeply.

He felt the first flux of warmth closing in around him, white light protecting him as always. Once again the invocations worked. He snuggled into his well-protected space and allowed them to come closer, waiting for them to connect like Soyuz docking at the space station with a mild jolt.

They squeezed in from all sides like a contracting sphere, like UFOs around the lone pilot over DC in nineteen fifty-two, the manifestation of their incorporeal intelligence palpable. Many or one? Who was coming? He couldn't tell. He felt a telltale pressure in his brain, the hair on the back of his neck bristling. He shivered with excitement: this was the phase when they calibrated their intentions to his receptivity, testing his readiness. They needed to lower their vibrations, come down in syncopated steps to his level, while Bobby honed his receptors, refining the grosser elements of his mind. They were both, as it were, turning dials, tuning in to each other. Now he extended the internal mechanism, unfolding at the edges, making himself open to their probe.

He reached out with mental energy, feeling...

... a light touch. Yes. Then, very gently, coupling.

Hey, Bobby J! Here we are!

His hand without the hand-moving part of his mind so much as moving, started to move. The pencil point drew loops as the spirits moved into closer control of an apparatus they were still learning to manipulate. The loops and whirls grew closer, denser, darkening the page. Suddenly the pencil paused; he inhaled deeply, letting them settle. Delicate, this adjustment was. He had to get out of the way or nothing would happen. This required courage, they explained, not control but on the contrary letting go, letting the spirits move into his body and brain, his body/brain they called it, which they described with elegant mathematical precision from the multidimensional perspective they apparently inhabit all around.

The pencil began to write slowly, then faster and faster. The instrument (that is, Bobby J) was imperfect. "But," they explained, "You're what we have. You of all people on this planet have been chosen because you are perfectly suited to our task. You must proclaim our message to the world. You are an aperture, narrow and defective, yes, but still, a means of deliverance — if you obey. Your destiny has been set from all time and eternity. You have been prepared for this moment from birth. Before birth, in fact. We attended your development in the womb. Do you remember that your mother was sick in the fifth month? Yes? No? Well, she was. Yet she — and you — survived. <flutter of a chuckle in the shadows of his mind> Yes, Bobby J, that was us, ensuring your safe delivery.

You could ask her, if she hadn't passed through.

"We will illuminate your path, and you will see that things you believed accidental were in fact achieved by design and with our help. You will see your future before you like golden footsteps into the darkness – but you will see as well the price you must be willing to pay. That price will be revealed over time as you become capable of understanding and embracing your fate.

"Do not be afraid. We will be with you and give you what you need."

"Accept this message with gratitude."

Bobby tried not to let his ego swell which they warned him would interfere with their plan. He grinned inside his head each time they showed him to himself as he would become, as he already was, they explained, in a future state that already existed, letting him see clearly who he was and who he was meant to be. What human would not bloat with self-importance, seeing the unique role he would play in the cosmic drama? With discipline, however, and their assistance, his ego could be held in check.

"You must become small, oh smaller, you must become smallest of all to do this work."

The pencil – that was Trance 14/December 17– wrote gibberish after that, words obscuring words until the paper was a mess. He scrutinized it later in the bright kitchen light but couldn't make sense of anything.

"Don't be anxious if some messages are lost," they had said in Trance 7B/October 23. "We will repeat anything of importance. The monitor of this process, after centuries of preparation, is quite adept."

He was letting them in now, letting himself surrender, moving into a deeper state. His head fell forward. Bobby J belonged to them now; letting them work out their higher purpose through his slouching body, chin on chest. He gave himself up for the greater good, aware that his body/brain was a channel for the correction of a planet unaware of its peril. Catastrophe was imminent unless an intervention took place, and that right soon. And Bobby J was the means of intercession.

The pencil wrote across one page and then another. His left

hand shuffled fresh pages to his right which scribbled words he neither saw nor understood until he read them later — words of great spiritual power, words of encouragement, words of wisdom.

Sometimes their messages illuminated the essential nature of things. Sometimes they told deep truths of the multidimensional universe, how it worked, although the details were not always consistent. Sometimes their playful exchanges reminded Bobby J to have a sense of humor.

Sometimes they delivered gentle discipline to keep their pupil on track.

And sometimes... sometimes specific instructions were given that Bobby J learned had better be carried out.

Better be carried out, Mister. Better be carried out.

Or else.

Little Buster barked and barked, the goddamn little dog did not shut up, and on some level, despite his commitment to remain on the spiritual plane needed for the work, the incessant barking massively pissed off Bobby J, Servant of the White Light and a means of grace to unborn millions.

Alaracon, his primary guide, demonstrated compassion, his Cheshire-cat-like smile inner lit like a Halloween lantern.

"All truth must navigate a mine field of interruptions," Bobby's hand wrote without knowing it. "Life is lived via detours, but there are no dead-ends in fact. Everything is essential. Everything connects to everything else.

"That little dog is true to its nature. So must you, Bobby J, be true to yours, to our teaching and to our invitation."

Little Buster's barking nevertheless pricked at Bobby's trance and awakened his ego-consciousness. He felt himself rising through levels of awareness toward the surface of his life. He felt as if he were moving through thermoclines into warmer surface waters. His hand wrote more slowly, then made loops and squiggles, then stopped. He held the pencil for a moment more, then let it fall. It rolled off the wooden table and dropped to the floor. His head came up at the sound and he opened his eyes.

The candles had burned down and only a few flickered, their wicks in pools of melted wax. Bobby shivered, feeling the chilly room for what it was, an empty apartment, a bodyless tomb. When the spirits departed it felt like good friends leaving. He rose stiffly from the table and blinked rapidly, trying to calibrate to the physical plane. Paper covered with illegible inspired script was all over the table and a few sheets had fallen to the floor. He walked around them to the window and looked out. For a moment a medieval village so it seemed slept under a blanket of snow. Time displacement, time dilation? No. He rubbed his eyes, closed them for a moment, looked again: the familiar city street reappeared, West Byron Street in a neighborhood going through gentrification, twiddling its run-down thumbs to the sound of wrecking balls, jack-hammers, and impotent protests from those who had to move.

Parked cars looked like loaves of snow and streetlights burned without heat in the winter night. Not a creature stirred, not even Little Buster; the ratty terrier had stopped barking at last, probably eating his owner's slippers, maybe the sofa. The sidewalk below had disorganized holes stomped in the deep snow by somebody's boots and where the girl had tumbled into the snow bank the snow was disheveled. Maybe she tried to make an angel in the snow. Maybe some guy pushed her down. Maybe she slipped.

Across the street on the corner, in a retail strip too brightly lighted for this silent night, a luminous two-faced clock on a neighborhood bank proclaimed the time. Bobby chuckled. The time by which his species marked off days was irrelevant to the scheme. Whatever the time, it was neither wrong nor right. It was also wrong and right, they said. Then they would laugh together, pretending what they said made sense.

"Yes, you must become acquainted with the night," his guides had instructed (the spirits liked Frost, Wordsworth and Eliot a lot, quoting them more than other poets). "To become a warrior of the light one must brave the darkness. One must navigate a zone of annihilation before one can read luminous letters written in script in the night-blue sky. Only then will you know that you have reached the far shore. Only then can you choose when and how to return."

Bobby twisted his head to try to look up through the window. Moon and stars were hidden by an overcast sky. Citylight reflected from the snow and back down from low clouds. The scene was inside a snow globe waiting for someone to shake it. Bobby J felt suddenly as lonely as he ever had in his life. He felt as lonely as Holden, as lonely as Gary Webb when he found his motorcycle stolen. He yawned and stretched and realized he was hungry. He heard faint laughter through the bedroom wall which meant someone was watching a monologue, Colbert's or Fallon's. He had been gone a long time. Yawning more, he walked into the kitchenette and searched the fridge, finding cold pizza in a plastic baggie. He put it into the microwave on a paper towel and, while it turned in the microwave merry-go-round, went back and carefully assembled the drifted pages in an order which sort of made sense. Then returned to the kitchen and read the first page by the dim light of the microwave.

"It is time to begin your training. [huh? I thought that happened long ago.] We have given you the parameters of your mission. Now you must demonstrate yourself able of execution." [capable?] You must be disciplined. Able to follow instructions. Be attentive under any and all. [circumstances? situations? what?] Watch our hands waitfully as a good sub waits upon his mistress. Be compliant, Bobby J. Be a good bottom. Be willing to do what we say when we say it. Delay your own pleasure. Willing to let whatever. Act always as if.

"This is the hour of your knitting [knitting? knighting? what the hell did that mean?]"

The light went off and the motor stopped. He opened the oven, burning his fingers on bubbling crackling cheese. "Damn!" he said, sucking his fingers, then scooping up the square of paper towel fused with melted cheese, hitting the overhead light in the other room and sitting to eat.

He ate around the edges of an amalgam of paper-and-pizza while he read.

"The circles of intersecting levels of planetary influence are many — many to our eyes although we do not have eyes we are like eyes we are like wise alive eyes all-wonderful beings. We see far. The many the much that we see seems few to you because you see say red blue yellow and do not know that infra red and ultra violet much less radio or x-rays or the longer ones whatever the names even exist. We see the entire spectrum and struggle to say in your small frame what it looks like to you little cave fish blind in subterranean streams but infinite to us.

"You are like a walking fish barely out of the mud. You are so recently arrived at the first rung. You think feebly and dream worse. That is not an insult, Bobby J. That is simply what's so."

[what are your bodies like? his higher entity-self asked]

"Everything will be revealed. We can tell you now that all bodies are apertures through which light shines or is eclipsed, depending. Each illumines according to its frequency. Each designed to amplify and modulate a particular frequency. We see the entire spectrum because we are between high and even higher forms and lower grosser forms like you. Your species scrabbles at the bottom of the pond in detritus. If we manifested in your part of the spectrum we would seem to you translucent, gelatinous like jellyfish in water-cage in Monterrey, we would be diaphanous, glowing with inner light. We would seem to you beautiful but you would miss the overall."

[are there higher beings than you?]

[laughter in many dimensions sounding a lot like munchkins hiding while the good witch, fresh from her bubble, helpfully clarified]

"Oh yes! Yes! We are barely little more than thus. There are realms of beings communing one with another in outwardly bounding links or loops. We are what some call messengers or angels or spirits. But that is not our essence. That is not who we are. That is how you fit us into myths. We are fashioned —"

Bobby let the paper go and used both hands to separate the messy paper from the pizza. It seemed an apt analogy for trying to find nourishment in the crumbs they dropped through multiple dimensions.

He read their expository passages over and over again, searching the obscure repetitious text for clarity and meaning. He longed for a map illuminating the universe instead of fragments, in part because he craved to begin teaching. They insisted that his actions would demonstrate his knowledge and they would know when he was ready. But Bobby wanted more: he wanted his first brave actions to seem like the miracles he thought they were while he alone knew they were causal events in a rule-based universe, the levers of which he knew how to use. Once people understood what he did, they would listen. The miracles were merely to get attention, a barker drawing a crowd before a fire-eater turned the tip.

Not like now. Now, no one listened. He sent the revelations, edited with care, to magazines and papers but they never appeared. He put some on a web site but received no hits. He wrote a blog called Voice of the White Light but no one read it. He began Facebook pages dedicated to spreading the word but no one liked them, everyone avoided them, refusing to be his "friend." He tweeted the fruits of his genius but no one followed him, not a one. He created three avatars (Disciple of the White Light, Friend of Alaracon, Bobby J) in Second Life, but no one listened to his preaching.

This is to be expected, they explained. "Thus has it always been," Alaracon said. "Thus will it always be. Prophets without honor and all that claptrap."

Every rejection renewed his dedication and reinforced his belief in his mission and he plunged into the universe, understood as a recursive structure like Escher's etchings or Godel's theorems, one that paradoxically required one to be inside to gain entry. Which is where he was, he thought. Which felt however like a prison on a long dark winter night.

Whenever he had almost attained a higher level, he found himself sliding back to a level he thought he left behind. The universe turned into a game of chutes and ladders, one he could never win. When he expressed frustration, his guides' munchkin laughter crackled like static in his brain, giving him a headache. Again and again they explained that when he had grown to the appropriate level, that recursive slide to GO would cease, he would find himself standing on the top rung of a ladder in a way that seemed astonishing, oh the delicacy of his balance, then the ladder would vanish and he would remain suspended, platform and dancer, figure and ground, and then he would understand... *everything.*

But first, they said, the journey. Then the oasis. You must learn, Bobby J, when to hold and when to fold. When to raise and when to walk walk walk away away a way a way...

Their fading voices ricocheted in his brimming brain. Then a final remark:

"This is Big Toy time, Bobby J, so learn how to climb. Next will come Big Boy time when you fly.

"So forgive us, beloved disciple, for what must seem repetitious. These are your multiplication tables. This is drill. Transcribe faithfully. Study without ceasing. You are like young Luke on Tatooine, we are like little Yodas, smiling, kindly and wise. We are waiting for you to learn, and as Yoda said, there is another. And there is. On this planet too, we mean. There is another, honestly. Meanwhile, you must do, not try. With tough love must we train our pupil. Not for nothing have we come."

Bobby J sighed. Thanks, guys. That really helps.

He reread the pages, sorted and stacked them and punched holes and put them into a binder. His book was getting thick. Ragged pages crinkled from repeated readings, so many passages meaningless from scrawl or smear, interpretive translations neatly printed in ink between the lines using words he hoped were analogous or close.

The pages that intrigued him most were links and loops, linking and looping, Jackson Pollock-sort-of-like, schematics delivered as their voices faded — in which, he was certain, images and symbols conveyed the inexplicable splendor of white and gold, a representation of the universe, the multiverse, whatever it was, and how it worked, the master plan, they slyly implied, of… every-existing-thing.

That vision gave him vertigo. He felt like fainting. Fear throttled his heart which pounded loudly and he hugged himself tightly, afraid he would fall. Perspiring profusely, he raced to get into his parka, pulled his woolen cap down onto his forehead, tightened the drawstrings of the gray-blue hood and hurried downstairs to the street.

The still windless night waited, a few large flakes of softly falling snow in the quiet sky and drifting snow all around. Faraway sounds were absorbed by the snow, quieting the city. The distant rumble of an elevated train. Then a snow plow scraping snow into banks along parked cars came loudly down the avenue into the empty intersection and disappeared with a soft Doppler fade to the west.

Bobby shoveled out his auto and slid through the slippery streets to the Stop-n-Go. Lakshman Noorkhan nodded silently inside his glass cube when he entered. Beef and pepperoni sticks, cigarettes and beer, hot cashews in a brightly lighted glass display, freshly popped popcorn, old-fashioned doughnuts, elephant ears, éclairs, apple fritters, pershings, donut holes and vadas, all competed for his cash. The radio was low and played nothing he knew. It sounded like a sitar. The Indian looked out at the world patiently and waited.

"How fresh are those doughnuts?"

"Fresh?" He shrugged. "Today. Very fresh."

"Uh-huh," Bobby said. Looking around at candy bars, swizzle sticks, rows of flashy wrap and crinkly see-through packaging. He looked at a peanut butter cookie full of chocolate chunks and almost bought it. But someone said or thought no. Instead he said, "I'll take two of those fritters."

The Indian used tongs to take two puffy fritters flaking with icing and put them into a paper bag. Bobby slid exact change through the slot and said thanks. The proprietor put the bag in the drawer and the doughnuts surfaced on Bobby's side.

Bobby J ate the first one standing there, flexing his cold toes on rubber matting covered with slush. He smelled strong Lysol from the store room and washroom. Reminded him of peep shows. He looked closely at the guy behind the glass, a man he had seen a million times, but never saw the look in his eyes or expression on his face. He had seen only an impassive brown face with dark eyes. Now he saw Lakshman Noorkhan, an Indian from a real town beside some river, more than that, he saw a man. He saw a human being.

The contours of the man's anonymous life shifted into closer focus. Like desert turning into hills and growing grass in a program that made things morph, Lakshman Noorkhan became three dimensional.

Bobby knew who would take credit. Then he heard them laugh and felt a push.

Still, he waited, resisting the nudge. Sure enough, they were at the Stop-n-Go, they were everywhere, they were inside the fritter, inside his body/brain. Yes, they wanted him to, *now!* He resisted again, looking at the stuff on the shelves, not really seeing. Halfway there and halfway back, he made them press. *Speak now, Bobby J: we insist that you speak, deliver the words* said a voicelet behind and to the right. But instead of fulfilling their request, Bobby moved up an aisle, jittering once more. Arms akimbo and legs quaking, looking silly in the digital film the owner would examine the next day, saying *what the fuck we get last night?* –he stared at hostess cupcakes, hohos, crumb cakes, donettes, boxes of donuts (plain cake, powdered sugar, chocolate chocolate, nutty ones), Twinkies and HoHos and lucky puffs, fruit pies (cherry peach and lemon), cinnamon rolls, coming around in front of a cooler holding sodas, sweet teas, juices, energy drinks, bottles of water into the next aisle, looking at twizzlers, jolly ranchers, chuckles and gummies, little snickers, Swedish fish, lemon drops and juju mix, night crawlers and gummy worms, caramels and peanut clusters, Mars bars, Snickers, Hershey bars, M&Ms of all kinds (peanut plain and almond, green and red and yellow and blue), trail mix and nibbles, chewies and licorice bits —

Goddamn it Bobby J! NOW!

"Mister, I don't know what you're after," Bobby said suddenly and forcefully to the Indian who started. "But I am supposed to tell you to hang in." He looked closely at the other's surprised features but saw more than surprise. "I can see how much you've suffered. It's a long winding road all right. You have traveled far and are uncertain of the rest. I can see that. And you miss whoever you left behind, I sense it is a woman, your age or maybe younger. But it won't always be like this. Something better is coming. Everything will come together. Please be patient and wait, It will arrive. The universe has wonderful things waiting downstream, more than you can imagine."

Lakshman Noorkhan tilted his head while the familiar but unknown customer spoke. He didn't know what to say to this young guy standing there among the candy and doughnuts with white icing on his mouth, looking at him so intensely and declaiming whatever came into his head. That was OK with Bobby J. He wasn't looking for a response. The thing is, his job is, deliver the message. That's all. Then, his anxiety diminished for a moment, responsibility fulfilled, he can go home.

The two men stared at one another in silence in the late night well-lighted shop. A bell rang when an auto drove over a signal hose, either a car or the voice of an angel singing in the night. Through the shadowy glass and his own reflection, Bobby watched a guy in a yellow-and-black plaid jacket and leather hat with flappy ears come in and give Noorkhan a twenty, then go back out to pump. A woman was driving, her face obscured by the icy night. All he could tell was she wore a dark parka with a hood around her pale face. The guy stayed out in the cold, pumping gas, playing a gent.

While Noorkhan inputted the twenty and set the pump to pump, Bobby rushed out and got back into his car and skidded off, eating the second fritter with one hand and fishtailing around a corner, heading back to his little apartment, no longer a cold tomb but a warm grotto in which twelve candles had burned down but in which the wicks nevertheless remained arranged in a twelve-wick circle surrounding the table in one of three apartments (1G, 2G, and 3G), only one of which, however (his!) had been touched by a vortex of energy funneled through a portal between or among dimensions (let those who have ears to hear, hear) in a night breaking free at last from its chains and exploding like Roman candles, sparklers of light igniting in the celebrating sky.

That wasn't the end, however. It was barely the beginning.

The next morning, Bobby Jakus applied for a job. He knew he had to, had known it for a long time. There was very little left of his pittance of inheritance. They told him to get a job last month. Then Alaracon said in a tone he couldn't ignore, get off your ass and do it. So he did.

The big black guy —"Call me Juicy Fruit," he said — looked at his application and laughed. "That a real name? Jakus?"

"No. I made it up."

The big guy thought about hitting the kid, not too hard, just knocking some sense into his fool head. Wake him the fuck up. Instead he said, "You think acting like an asshole will get you a job?"

Bobby remembered a lesson from the spirits and bit his tongue. Practice, they said. Practice being more human.

"No. I don't." He took a deep breath. This was a new behavior but he did it. "Sorry."

"Huh." It took the black man aback. But it worked. Interesting! "What you been doing? What was the last job you had?"

"My last 'job' job was working on a garbage truck. My current job is messenger."

"Yeah? Like on a bike?"

"In a way. I deliver communications, words of empowerment, hope, and encouragement, top-level wisdom, stuff like that. I illuminate the universe, as humans call it. They said I can say I'm a specialist in wisdom, but the insights are theirs. It's like I'm a tiny sphere inside a bigger sphere. On my own, not so much."

While Juicy Fruit was thinking about that, wondering should he tell him what it made him think, how he sounded perhaps a little bit nuts, Jakus surveyed the boiler room. The noise of machinery filled the underground cavern. They sat on torn vinyl chairs beside a scarred Formica table. Other chairs were scattered in shadows, a brown sofa with stuff on it too, mostly clothing. A couple of big pillows with indentations shaped to the big man's head. Old porn – magazines! - spilled from a stack on the floor beside the sofa. Jakus saw classics like Leg Show, Big Jugs, Hustlers, and right on top, Whiplash with a picture of a dom in red latex, maybe leather, he couldn't tell, with a crop in her hand. He tilted his head and read, *the tip of the toes to the top of the hose.*

Well, that made sense. As much as any trigger did.

We don't choose what we like. We like what we like.

He looked around. Naked bulbs burned in a crossgrid of pipes from which drops dripped to a stream that ran down the concrete floor to a drain. One steady drip dropped from a wet rag wrapped around the largest pipe. The big guy was sitting in a work shirt and torn jeans, his barrel chest bigger than Bobby's whole body, buttons straining, buttons stretched. The guy's huge hands dangling between his thighs. Not a guy to mess with, no one had to tell him that.

The door to the boiler room was open, letting him see a receiving desk, an empty shelf, a wire mesh screen between whoever came in and whoever was there, stairs going up to an outside platform. Nobody out there, near as he could tell. Nobody here but Juicy Fruit, living it appeared in the basement of the Berrigan Warehouse, lately redeveloped into lofts by Rupert Rapell and the Rapell Group.

The big guy said, "Look around. This is where we work, some of the time. I spend a lot of my time here, so I try to make it feel like home. We got quite a few different tasks, depending on weather. The four floors upstairs, those are apartments, condos, lofts, call them whatever. The fancier ones are on four, Rapell himself, the owner, he combined two into one with balconies all the way around. That's 404. His honey lives there now, this gal with black hair, you'll know her when you see her. Why he wants to look at an alley and a wall, who knows. That floor we do first. Floors three two one, it don't matter in which order, we do next, We clean the halls and back stairs at night or first thing in the morning. We don't vacuum in the morning because they cry about the noise. We got a couple of gentlemen on one who sleep all day and work all night on computer shit. So we humor them, we vacuum in the afternoon. After we do the stairs, we clean the hall.

"Next door, south, is an office, a real estate place on the bottom floor of offices, a couple of shops that sell sundries, whatever the fuck sundries are, the Rapell Group manages that too. Rapell does some rentals out of that office. He does all kinds of stuff that ain't our concern. Always something going on the side. We clean it three times a week, after they leave. Mister Rapell, he's the Man, he works at The Bank. He's always on the go. All we do is empty his baskets, lay vacuum tracks in the rug, empty ashtrays, shit like that. In the summer, we trim those bushes along the front, plant shit that never grows in this dirt, we mow whatever scraggly grass comes up and pick up trash that people drop like their mothers gonna come along, we clean up dog shit too, there's always some fucker letting his dog shit on the lawn. In the spring when the snow melts, there's dog shit and cigarette butts and cellophane paper. Our job is simple: clean it the fuck up. You be my assistant, you do what I say.

"Can you handle that?"

Bobby J said yes, "I can do that."

"You work three days a week in winter, four in summer. Pay is hourly, minimum wage whatever it is plus a buck. No benefits. You want it?"

Bobby sighed. His body/brain said no but they made his lips say yes. "I guess. When do I start?"

"Tomorrow morning. You work Tuesdays Thursdays Saturdays. Saturdays, we start at seven. Cool?"

Bobby looked at the big guy sitting on the too-small chair in his uniform shirt with his name written in threads, holes in his jeans' knees. The drip dripped nearby like a syncopated clock but the big guy was dry, out of the way.

"I'd prefer to start later."

"Yeah?" the big guy laughed. "Write that down, I'll give it to the union."

He laughed loudly until Bobby looked away.

"Like I say, start at seven." He looked him up and down. "Garbage truck. What did you learn on a garbage truck? How'd you get that job?"

"My mother knew the alderman from college. He set it up."

"Your momma, she know people like that?"

"No, she's dead. She died two years ago of cancer."

"Sorry to hear it. They all do. Your father? He connected?"

"No. He dropped dead when I was two. My mother went back to work at the place where he worked until she died too."

"Hm. Shit happens, don't it?"

"Yes."

"So the alderman, Rosenzweig you mean?"

"Yes. Abner Rosenzweig."

"You pay him back, do shit for him, come election time?"

"That was the deal."

"What he have you do? Knock on doors? Hand out shit?"

"That, and a bunch of other things. Everything was illegal. I gave voters money or booze, followed his competition and tore up stuff, helped the blind pull levers, lots of blind in our ward. I went door to door and learned what people needed too. That was the bottom line, what do you need? Then they provide it, when they can. Guys in business need a zoning change, guys making ends meet need this or that. If they need insurance for a business, they have to get it from him."

"You learned a lot right there. How the city works."

"Yeah, I did learn a lot. I learned that when the garbage truck hits the curb and you're standing up, hold on. I learned that if you fell in the garbage, just stay there, looking up at the sky and thinking to yourself, this isn't what it looks like, I'm just taking a ride. I did like bouncing down the street, even lying in the garbage, watching clouds and the tops of buildings. When I cut grass downtown, I learned to hide tools so if reporters came around they couldn't take a picture. They taught us where to go for long breaks, we took three, four hours at a time. This one guy, Frank, he drove the truck, he never once helped us lift the cans, going by union rules. Frank had a cottage on a little lake but all he did there, he said, other than watch football, was fuck Marie his wife."

"You ask him about stuff? Other stuff?"

"No, I never asked. I learned not to ask. That was one thing I learned. Like this one guy, Red? He was built like a brick shithouse, he collected loans on weekends for guys in a bar on Morgan, they told me not to fuck around with Red, but he was always nice to me. But then, I never borrowed money from his friends. He helped me, too. There was a guy always at the kiosk on Morgan and Thrush, selling papers. One day he wasn't there anymore. There was some new guy. I asked where the other one went, and the new guy shrugged. I asked Red what happened, and Red said, kid, don't mention that guy again. Keep your mouth fucking shut. He's gone. That's all there is to it."

"Good advice, you ask me."

"I guess. I learned to pay dues to a union that never had meetings. I learned to buy however many tickets to the mayor's games they told me to buy. I learned Ranger Rick in the City stuff, like where gays hang out, what rest rooms, what picnic tables they fuck on so you don't eat a sandwich on those. I learned about guys with cameras who hide and take pictures of anything. Any goddamn thing."

"People do like what they like."

"They do. One guy hid in the outhouse in the forest preserve, he stood there all morning in shit, wearing waders, waiting for women to sit above his face. Then he took pictures. He had his lunch with him in a brown bag. They found it when they chased him. A woman looked down through the hole and saw this guy and screamed and he climbed out and ran."

The big guy chuckled. "Yeah, they all around. Everybody into something."

He stretched his hands out in front of his stomach and cracked his knuckles. It echoed in the closed room, making a loud report. "Okay, then, Bobby Jakus, you know all kinds of shit. Then you won't be surprised by what goes on, upstairs. You see what people throw away, you know who they are. You see that Fischetti gal, anything she does, don't say a word."

"I understand."

"See, we're invisible, Bobby J, they pay us no mind. We're background. They see us when we make noise. We're like a highway, the only time they notice is when there's potholes. Then they scream."

Jakus smiled. "Alaracon says people think of him that way, too. Most people don't notice invisible hands, all around."

"Alaracon. Weird name. He a friend of yours?"

"I hope so. I sure hope so."

"Yeah, well, we need all the friends we can get." He stretched and yawned. "So be here at seven. Cool?"

The kid nodded.

You're an apprentice, Alaracon told him. That is the perfect job. We provide work that will teach you patience. You must learn to wait, Bobby J, until the right time. This is all prep for the Big Show. We want you ready when the moment comes.

<How long, oh friends, his higher mind cried, how long?>

Perhaps months, perhaps years, his reluctant hand wrote in a disappointed scrawl, part of his mind watching what another part did. But remember… we are with you always.

Then Clairon, a lieutenant or a lesser one, sang in a high unmistakable voice, do not sit on the edge of your chair, waiting for the bell. Sit back in the rocking chair of your soul. This is not a sprint. You are no neutrino, Bobby J, you are a proton and you look to us like an immense Midwest megapounder lumbering along.

Suddenly in the humid basement, rainbows surrounded the light bulbs as if he had been swimming in a chlorinated pool, and he thought he heard a sound like trumpets: "Yay!" they said, "You're a janitor's right-hand man, Bobby J! Good for you!"

As if it was something to celebrate.

It *is,* one insisted. It's perfect for learning to live small and be transparent to your purpose. This is how it begins, with a whimper. Most of the time, it ends with a whimper too.

We just report, Clairon said. We don't make the damn thing up.

"All right," Bobby said with a sigh, either to the spirits or Juicy Fruit, as he came around through the back door into his life. "I'll be here at seven."

CHAPTER 9
The Guy in the Blue Shirt

The day he arrived, the sky became dark early - night arrived in mid-afternoon after the false promise of a sunny morning — and his heart darkened too, as tired as he was, and dislodged from spacetime as he had known it, and challenged by the culture of the upper Midwest. Despite the momentary lift of meeting Heidi that morning and planning to meet her later, he waded through the afternoon, wanting the day to be done. It was well below zero, and the wind made it worse. So Teufel was pretty touchy when he went to the bank to get the key to his loft.

Everything had been arranged, all he had to do was go to The Bank, ask for Mister Pedamore, and get the key. It sounded simple. But first, he had to get past a gatekeeper, a woman who wanted a stop-and-chat. She must have been bored, he thought, spending her days at a desk near the elevator hall.

"I haven't seen a hat like that in years," said Roni Gersten, giving him a smile, showing she was joking.

"Oh?" said the guy, thinking he was insulted. He leaned toward her glass-topped desk, giving her an odd smile. She thought of a grin in a fun-house mirror, how it looked under his flappy hat, the flaps hanging loose. Nordic, she thought, not knowing that Bunny would classify him as that the minute she saw him at the shop. "Many people wear hats like this, back home." She thought he was kidding, too, unless by home he meant an asylum.

She forced a smile, making herself look as odd as he did. Mirroring folks was a large part of her job, picking up cues and giving them back. That made people think she liked them, in a way, and the space became transparent, neutral, difficult to leverage against her.

"Yah, you from the U.P.?"

A tallish-feeling Teufel took in her navy blue pants suit, her features cut from granite, wearing little makeup unless it was so well done it looked like none. He guessed she thought perspiration shining on her high forehead was sexy, her dark hair worn in a pixie cut with a little volume on top, a short spiky fringe and layered sides. He looked with undisguised distaste at a faint dark mustache.

Even with Roni Gersten down behind her desk, four feet tall in her chair, Teufel felt a need to lean into her personal space, respond to the challenge. He was not in a mood to buy bullshit, not that afternoon. It wasn't personal, it was business, the business of controlling the script, the narrative, creating a bit of tension. Then he could be funny unexpectedly, and the tension would break like a fever.

He curved into her space, feeling the edge of her desk on his thighs, and made sure he blocked her light, his shadow crossing her face, making her back up in her chair from the carpet onto the hard wood floor with a clunk.

That put her in light again, and Teufel pulled himself back, making himself taller, much taller, in his estimation, a guy who wasn't taking crap — a mask for his anxiety, which grew through the day as he tried to be human while remembering who he really was. The tenuousness of his memory was an additional stress. His identity in his cosmic home flickered in and out like a ghost. Anxiety laddered his chest like a trellis and he breathed deeply to settle down, in and out, in and out, watching her watch him watch her watch him, a quizzical look in her eyes, until he was under control. It took a while to get there, but he did. He wanted to give her a slap, the way she looked so superior, as if she was the boss of him, a flat hand to the right cheek, then a backhand when her head bounced — he had seen that move in Eastwood films and thought it was pretty cool. Make my day, he would say through compressed lips. He restrained himself, however, knowing there were cameras in the bank, as there were cameras everywhere, now, so others too were always on stage.

Being with us most when we know it not.

He worked his jaw, loosening tension. He looked like he was chewing a cud. Maybe his persona was a bit tight. He thought of the Bug pulling on his Elmer suit, the way his face twisted as he pulled the skin up. That's how he felt he looked, as if he was wearing a Teufel-suit. Needing to always be in charge was giving him a headache and even more anxiety, as the burden of his humanity sank into the pit in which he lived. The multiverse was immense and he was small — smaller than when he was part of the Skein. Of course, he still was, part of the Skein, but as a human, his knowledge of that was intermittent and diffused. So there was that then on top of it.

Roni Gersten couldn't believe the routine she was seeing, this flappy-hatted guy doing audible and visible deep breathing, looking at a vanishing point somewhere, making her wait as if he were performing. Which of course he was, layering his behaviors in great sweeps out to the cloud. In any case, his strategy worked on all levels: anxiety was a retro emotion relished in the Skein, where consciousness floated freely, unattached to having or wanting "things" the lack of which was the major cause — of anxiety, that is. It was an earth-based pathology which gave them nevertheless a vicarious thrill. It also calmed him down, when he stepped back and looked at himself, and he breathed more normally. He waited a minute to be certain. Yes, he was breathing nicely now. As if he hadn't a care in the world.

"You know," he said, "shaving *is* an option. Or what-do-you-call-them--depilatories."

"What?"

He gave her the grin. She waited, but it didn't go away.

"On some planets," he added, "hominids no longer use potions and lotions, the kinds that fill your shelves. Humans are obsessed with hair and skin. We have options, we have everything from lots of hair to hairless, from bald to hairy bears that some gays like. You know what I mean, the big burly guys covered with thick black mats."

Her brain couldn't process his comment. It didn't link to anything. Anomalies are like that. "You've got mail" rang twice but when she clicked, there was nothing there. Nothing links to nothing, click again.

He was still grinning, his smile etched in his facial plates, she thought she saw his skull beneath the skin. She had better say something, quickly too.

"I like that jacket, too, the Paul Bunyan look. You get that up Brainerd way?"

"No. That statue was not in Brainerd, you know. The guy with the ax is in Bathgate. Google can lie, I understand. Wikipedia's full of lies. But that's what it said, after the ads, when I finally got a real link. Brainerd is even less interesting than it seemed in that film." He smiled widely, reminding Roni of The Joker. "That sheriff was a rare character for them. Warm and toasty and easy to love. I do my homework, you know. I am no fool."

"No, I'm sure you aren't." She thought of Max Bialystok looking at the camera when Leo chewed the scenery. "Brainerd is less interesting than... what? how it sounded in a film? Or less interesting than talking to an immigrant? From another planet, shall we say?"

Teufel stared. Where the fuck did *that* come from? How did she know? Was information leaking from one bubble to another? Was the intensity of the moment making them matter to each other, so data moved through the translucent membranes between their brains? The way a person appeared to another at the moment of death?

"Hmm..." (he said, thinking, what do I say?) "Hmm. Yes. A new planet can be interesting, even a primitive one. Would you like a soliloquy, then, as if I were from a different planet?"

In for a dime, in for a dollar. "Sure," she said.

"OK. This planet amuses the Skein. You would call the former denizens 'species,' using your taxonomies, but you must know, they are incorrect the minute you make them up. Because they are always morphing. The gene pool is fluid. And once species link, no one is the same any more, they become something else. On top of that, once we take the reins into our own hands and drive uplift with intention, mutations become more frequent. Then we can pick and choose. The process accelerates. But the universe no longer plays dice, not the way it did, because we make the dice. We make the rules. We make the game. You would realize that if you gave it some thought. Consciousness can do all that, when it knows what it is."

He had spoken himself into boldness and Roni in fact was rapt. She felt like she was watching an accident happening in slow motion.

"Humans put on a good show. You are like a *New Yorker*, full of cartoons — and one-liners, take my wife, please — you are like SNL but funnier and more consistent. Some species are more primitive, believe it or not, but not many. Below your threshold of awareness, it drops off quickly into a flickering, than into mere potential. It's harder for hominids, because of brain plates, which cause interference. Insectoids exchange data in ways that scale well so when they leap, they land. Their buzzing is multi-channel, multi-valent — if, a big if, they transcend chemicals. That's why they are so abundant. Hominids require tweaking as your lot did. We gave the Sumerians a leg up, once, twice, three times a bene-fice, and what did it get? A dead culture, bequeathing nothing. Even now, you think Newtonian, long after you were told about spacetime! How can you get to five-D when you can't even think four? How can you live vibrantly? How can you free your minds?"

He sighed. "I do miss language streaming on all channels! It is not about 'strings.' Strings are non-starters. That idea made us laugh, our laughter was all around, but you never heard a murmur, did you? See, what sounds to you like tinnitus is in fact complex multi-channel chitchat, or hysterical laughter, or back-channel back-scratching politics, all at the same time. Politics is a name for adjustments among various perspectives. Although sometimes of course what you hear *is* tinnitus." Roni was turning pages of the DSM in her head. His rant made her brain race but also made a kind of sense. It was like atonal music — but she preferred Rachmaninoff.

"Do go on."

"Gladly! Humans think three or four things at most. You don't understand "body/brain." It's all one thing. You think you are here now when you are in fact entangled here and there. Think of Lawrence, taking the guy out of the tent and pointing. It's only a matter of going, he said. Oh, how right he was! Although I do not mean Aqaba, of course. I mean what is right there." He pointed to the elevator hall. "There. Right there."

The bank woman stared, her mouth open a little, then a lot, showing her teeth. She seemed confused, maybe in awe of his fluent explanations of how things are. He didn't know if she was following or just doing her job, sitting and smiling and acting more than he was.

They engaged in silence, then, eyes entangled, searching for room to maneuver or say something more. The silence was like a bell jar or the strangeness of a close encounter. There was no noise, until he spoke again and then they were back in familiar space time, with the whirring of fans and footsteps in the hall.

"I am curious, do you insult customers as a rule? Are you often rude, just for fun? To liven up your day?"

She blinked. She showed a blank face. Then looked away. She seemed more genuine, at any rate, without a false smile.

She pulled in her chair and looked for another conversational route. Dealing with guys like Teufel made her fretful, and then she got silly, defensive, making up stuff to make a burlesque and avoid what felt like a threat. These days, she often went into farce mode with Jimmy too — Jimmy Two, Jimi One. She didn't know what to call him anymore. But that was because of what he was doing. What was he doing anyhow? She didn't know.

She didn't know.

If she went later to see the rent-a-cop downstairs and asked to see the video, That's him, she would say, pointing to the surveillance camera image. No, he wasn't threatening in that way. He was unnerving. Show me more.

Videos showed Teufel approaching the bank, looking at the door, then at a paper in his hand, unsnapping the flaps of his hat, looking left, looking right, turning to look behind, then entering the foyer where another camera picked him up, asking the guard where so-and-so worked, the rent-a-cop at the lobby desk picking up a phone and calling upstairs. He asked his name, got an okay, and told him, "Twelve." Teufel went to the elevators where a third camera grabbed him, showing him pacing, rubbing his shoulder under the backpack strap. He watched numbers blinking in sequence, counting down, then he was hidden by a businessman getting off, then he went in, the camera in the elevator showing him watching numbers as if they were of interest. The elevator stopped on seven and a woman had to walk around him — Marta, from credit cards, going to lunch, pushing the up button by mistake. She stood behind him, showing nothing much. Then the video showed him getting off on twelve, looking left and right at the doors, picking one, and coming to Roni's desk.

"Let us know if he comes back," Gumbo said.

"OK. Thanks. But he didn't do anything, it was his manner —"

"I hear ya," Gumbo said, "and if they had picked up on their 'manner' at the marathon, we wouldn't have people with artificial legs, would we?"

He didn't get it, she thought. He was a hammer and everything was a nail. It was not like he was dangerous in the usual way. It was more like the landscape wavered as if you were looking through waves of heat. It was more like a door was ajar and something was behind it, waiting to spring.

"Well," Roni said "What can I do for you, Mister — ?"

"Teufel. Yes, let's do business. I arranged to rent an apartment using craigslist. The email came from a man at your bank named Rupert Rapell. He owns the apartment, condo, loft, whatever the fuck it is, but the man I need to see is his servant, Mister Larry Pedamore. He is a vice president."

"Larry. Right. OK then. Look over there," she nodded behind and he turned to look. "See those doors? The ones you came through?"

"Of course. My eyesight is quite good."

"Go through those doors, then through the ones on the other side of the hall. See that balding portly gentleman at the first desk on the left? — tell him you want to see 'the guy in the blue shirt.' He'll know who you mean."

"The guy in the blue shirt."

"Yes. Ask for the guy in the blue shirt."

Teufel hefted his backpack onto his shoulder, letting it hang by a strap, and made his way through the doors, the backpack bumping his shoulder blade, into a large fluorescent-and-window-lighted room with desks in long lines that disappeared into infinity, an immense cubicle city. It looked like it was made with special effects. Daylight filtered through low clouds and made the florescent light paler. Rectangular windows framed windows across the street. He looked down through the window at daylight diffusing as it fell through the high-rise canyon, dimming as it drifted, a shadow of itself by the time it reached the street.

At the first desk on the left was an outsized guy in his forties, hard to tell with guys of a certain age and weight and not a lot of hair, in a dark blue suit, a white shirt, and a striped tie. He looked up from his computer, tilted at an angle so Teufel couldn't see, even when he peeked, as he did, leaning around the monitor which the guy turned away so he couldn't see it even more, as if his data was a big fucking deal. The guy was dressed like everybody else, but looked disheveled. His white shirt bellied like a spinnaker, his buttons tight. The waistband turned over on his belt so he had to straighten it when he rose. His face glistened with perspiration in the flat light. His eyes were dull, his hair thin, what hair he had which wasn't much, and the skin of his head shone through his Trump-like comb-over.

"I am looking for the guy in the blue shirt."

The man stiffened. He stared at Teufel for a good half minute. Teufel was amused by his discomfort.

"She told you to say that, didn't she?"

"Yes. Did I say it wrong?"

"No. How could you know? That she thinks she is funny?"

"What is funny about asking for the guy in the blue shirt? You are wearing a white shirt, an older style but appropriate I imagine in this place. Although it does not fit, really. I don't understand. Help me out."

"Do you think she's funny?"

"Me? No," Teufel shook his head. "I would say she tends toward being controlling. But most humans do, one way or another. You evolved to think everything is a threat. So you play defense. But like you said, how would I know? I have no way to understand. To be funny, you need a context. You must understand the culture and its contradictions. Otherwise how is something funny? There is nothing to contrast with what this woman said, that I know, after our brief exchange. I think she needs a shave, she has a little dark mustache which I don't think is attractive on a woman, even a woman like her. But is she funny?" He shrugged. "How would I know?"

The guy in the white shirt leaned forward and looked through the glass doors. Teufel turned to see. In the distance, Roni was watching, laughing at making them look. She waved with a gleeful sweep of her arm.

"So what is the joke? She looks like she thinks it is pretty funny."

The guy slumped back and looked up at Teufel.

"Have you ever worked in a bank?"

"No. Why? Is it fun?"

"Fun? Oh, my, yes, working in a bank is the most fun a guy can have. I highly recommend working in a bank to anyone with an adventuresome spirit. It's more fun than a water park and less slippery. But that's not the point. Would you like to know the point?"

"Sure," Teufel said. "I am eager to learn how humans think."

"You mean other humans, right?"

Teufel shrugged. "Whatever."

The guy was breathing heavily, perhaps he was asthmatic, or merely obese, there was so much in the news about obese humans. "My first day of work, I wore a gray suit, a maroon tie, and a light blue shirt. I went to a meeting and everybody stared. Sometimes they nudged one another and whispered. I excused myself and checked everything — my fly was closed, my dick wasn't out, my buttons were buttoned, the tie hung plumb, as plumb as it could —"

Teufel laughed, looking at the flabby belly behind his desk. His tie went down for a bit, then angled out, away.

"Afterward, I sat in my cubicle — I was in a cubicle then, I hadn't moved up to a desk — and watched them walk by and look and giggle. By late afternoon, I figured it out."

"They had actually given a job to a straight white male?"

"What? No, no. What I realized, see, was that every man in the bank was wearing a white shirt. Every single one. Dark suit, long-sleeve white shirt with cuffs showing, and a dark tie. It was a uniform. But no one told me."

"They must have thought you were smart enough to do your homework, as in fact I had to do to come here," Teufel said. "I used the internet, movies. When was this?"

"Eighteen years ago."

"Ah. You did not have the benefit of cable or internet. Was it a casual Friday, perhaps? They expected you to be in jeans?"

"No. But that's not the point. The point is, that was eighteen years ago."

"So you said."

"Yes, and I have worn a white shirt every day. But do you know what they call me behind my back?"

Teufel shook his head. "Jabba the Hutt? Haystacks Calhoun?"

"Ho ho, another comic. No," he said, "they call me the guy in the blue shirt. Eighteen years later, they still call me the guy in the blue shirt."

"So that was the joke, then? when she said, ask for the guy in the blue shirt?"

"Yes. That was the joke."

"I see," Jack said. "She breaks your balls. And you take it. You are no Michael Corleone telling Kay you'll keep the kids. You sit there like a punching bag and go ropa-dope on life. Look what it did to Ali, a mumbling stumbling shadow of his former self."

Teufel shook his head. He felt genuine sadness.

"You poor sad fuck. I mean, working in a place like this must kill the inner beast. You do all kinds of stupid shit and make dumb jokes like she did just to get through the day. You endure abuse, humiliation, insolence and contumely, passive aggressive hostile pricks, the derision of bosses and customers. Your job review must be a joke. Nothing but doubletalk, yes? Bullshit this and bullshit that? Anything to avoid giving you more money. But you have a title, right?" he gestured to the nameplate. "They make you VP of some shit or other, and why not? It costs nothing. They still pay you little and on top of that, they break your balls. Meanwhile, at the top, they are criminals, yes? I did my home-work, Pedamore. They launder money for everyone, drug cartels, dictators, purveyors of illicit arms. But they write the laws, so they pay a fine if caught and that's that. Has a white male banker in a two-thousand-dollar suit ever gone to jail? No. You know who goes to jail? Nigger stickup men, Karen. Those bastards commit felonies by the bushel, insider trading, bond fraud, mortgage fraud, offshore laundering, manipulating rates of currencies and things. But when they're caught, they pay a fine, a cost of doing business. They cook the books like all the corporations and fuck guys like us in the ass. Assume the position, they say, now now, over the railing you go, mister normal ordinary person, that is, you poor powerless schmuck. Then they wipe their dicks on your pants. This is a zoo, one big circle jerk, a city of bonobos beating each other off to get through the day. But you call it 'a career' to deny the truth of your lives." Teufel looked around at desks and windows, windows without end, personal items propped on top of cubicles, photos of families, plastic flowers, football pennants, and gave a wide sweep of his arm, forcing Pedamore to sit back, "I have been here ten minutes and I get it. This place would make a person nuts. You must want to scream like the blonde in the shower — which was, really, a wonderful scene. That fat bastard loved torturing blondes. He made Kim Novak get into the cold water again and again long after he had the shot. He loved the pain on her face. And the girl in *The Birds* getting pecked? He got off on that all right. I mean, whoa daddy!"

The vice president of whatever smiled. He was used to hearing a lot of shit, and this wasn't that different from most. "Well. I don't know I'd say it like that, but it is sad, I agree. Over time, we lose confidence and don't think of taking risks. If we try to be creative, the hammer domes down."

"Yet banks run the world. Here in the upper Midwest, they say it is good for banks to be boring."

"Yes. But for good reason —"

Teufel laughed. "You minimize your pain. You drink Kool-ade, spill it all over yourself, it is not perspiration staining your shirt, although there is some too. This must be the place where dreams come to die like elephants in their burial grounds. It's very sad. You hear your dreams trumpeting as they disappear into the forest. I saw that on Discovery, I myself have never seen an elephant.

"I am amazed you don't shoot each other. Honestly, it should be called going banker, not going postal."

The guy in the white shirt laughed. "That would fix things, wouldn't it? Killing one another?"

Teufel nodded. "It might. It would certainly liven the series. Although it is hard to compete with all the other violence. Or the news. If it bleeds it leads."

His earnestness made the V-P chuckle.

"So... pleasant chitchat aside, what can I do for you?"

"Are you Larry Pedamore?"

"I am."

"OK then. You were sent rent and a security deposit via paypal. For a loft that Rupert Rapell wanted to rent. It was on craigslist. The message I received said you are the go-to guy. I assume someone did not spoof headers and send pictures of a false loft, that the one with the big windows, natural brick, a granite kitchen counter like I see on cable, plenty of exposed plumbing, everything one needs for an urban adventure is not a phish."

Pedamore smiled, "Ah, you're..." he opened a drawer and took out a file. "Jack Teufel."

"I am."

"Everything's set. I'm doing this as a favor for Mister Rapell. He's my boss, in the bank, but this is on the side. He does lots of things on the side. Here are keys and the lease," he handed him an envelope. "This is a sublet, you understand?"

Teufel nodded.

"Mister Rapell's name is not on the lease. He is doing this for his friend. The loft belongs to Carrie Fischetti who is moving to the top floor."

Teufel smiled. "Is she by any chance related to Charlie Fischetti? He was not on *Boardwalk Empire* but his boss was."

Pedamore shrugged. "I have no idea. She's your neighbor now, ask her. She works upstairs, down the hall from Mister Rapell."

"That would be something. Charlie Fischetti. Wow." Teufel

took the papers, glanced at the meaningless words, and signed on marked lines.

"The Berrigan Warehouse is on —"

"I know where it is. I use Google Maps. Maybe Apple map is better now but I do not want to walk into the river."

"You can grab a taxi —"

"I prefer walking. It acclimates me to the streets. I am getting a feel for the air as well, breathing it straight. I leave the bank to the west, turn right, then left and right again and go north. I will know the building by its facade and the alley along the side. The Berrigan is adjacent to a building with glass walls. There is a box-ing gym to the left and a real estate office to the right."

"Yes, that's the office to call if you have issues. Rapell preferred I handle this here, but there's a helpful Greek guy —"

"Fine, fine. I am eager to get going, if you don't mind."

"OK. Walk if you like, but it's cold out there."

"Baby it's cold outside. Is that what you want to say?"

Pedamore laughed. "You have an unusual sense of humor, Mister Teufel."

"Thank you. OK then," Teufel said. They looked at each other for a moment. "So that's that?"

"That's that."

The VP rose and shook hands with the new tenant, saving Rapell a lot of hassle by taking care of it quietly.

In the elevator hallway, Teufel looked at Roni Gersten who waved and smiled. He ignored her, turning his back.

Time enough for you, he thought.

And added her to his list.

Roni Gersten watched him wait for the elevator, pacing. The

backpack must have been heavy, the way it shifted on his back. The hat flaps curled up from his ears like little wings. She watched him fasten the leather strap, flap to flap, and button his yellow-and-black plaid jacket, then vanish into the elevator.

He reappeared downstairs and stepped from the lift. He stopped to watch a fountain in the lobby. Jets sprayed in bursts over a basin and loops of falling water made pools that quickly drained. Very cool. Through a glass wall, an outdoor patio was covered with snow. He imagined tables and chairs in summer. Bare winter trees were limned with snow. Knee-high evergreen shrubs arranged around the patio, loaded with snow. Across the street, another high-rise office building, windows higher than he could twist his head to see. He thought he heard the wind but it might have been the vents.

Through the glass, he watched pedestrians wait at the corner for the light. Flakes of snow drifted randomly down the canyons. A woman in a black coat, her cheeks coloring in the cold, shifted her weight as she waited, a man beside her, his hands in his over-coat pockets, hunched down with a turned-up collar. They did not seem aligned or allied.

The light changed and they curved their bodies into the stiff wind, crossing the street.

He looked around. A woman sold coffee at a cart, cappuccinos, lattes, americanos, mochas. Pastries were behind the glass — cinnamon buns, apple fritters, carrot cake, muffins, scones, he was hungry abruptly for them all. He forced himself to turn away and hurried into a circular glass door. Exiting into the cold, he burrowed into the wind and walked north, feeling as if he were wading in an icy river. As he walked he looked around, taking in the landscape, getting benchmarks for what they called normal.

People waited for buses, sheltering in doorways. The air smelled as if it was burning; the sky was tinged with smoke. He felt flakes of snow on his eyelids and looked up at large soft flakes floating between buildings, the snowfall making him feel as if he were in a snow globe, waiting for someone to shake it. The light snow muffled sounds around him. The city in his head went to sleep.

When he reawakened to the day, he knew he had gone off somewhere, into another space, unaware of what he had passed. But he must have turned at the right streets, for there it was, up ahead, the Berrigan Warehouse, four floors of brick with new iron balconies. A bicycle on one was covered with a tarp. The tarp in turn was covered with snow. The building looked as it had on the street view on Google. He leaned back and looked up at the sky which was bright with a mother-of-pearl light. Flakes of snow continued to drift down past sheer brick walls and disappear on the bare walk.

He took out his keys, opened the door, and dragged his backpack up the steps, though an inner door and down the hallway to his new home.

Inside, shades were up and a dim light filled the chilly space. He located the thermostat and raised the temp ten degrees. Then he claimed the territory, prowling his cage like a cat.

He dumped everything from his duffle onto the floor of his bedroom. He pushed on the bed, piled high with decorator pillows, and felt the appropriate give of a new mattress. He noticed empty dresser drawers, inviting him to fill it and make the place his own. He carried clothes from his duffle and dumped them into the drawers. He looked at the white inviting bed and wanted to nap but had to meet Heidi after she finished work. He checked the bathroom instead which, as the photo had showed, had a rain forest shower head and huge glass stall.

To stay awake, he watched TV but dozed to the drone of Doctor Phil. He awoke with a start. The light was almost gone, it was twilight time. Heavenly shades of night, and all. That strange half-awake daze, until he saw the clock.

Damn! Heidi would wonder where he was. He had better get going.

But first, he sat stiffly and moved his head back and forth. He searched for a signal but heard only noise. He closed his eyes and waited. Nothing came. Nothing filtered through. He was on his own. He would take his cues from the world, which meant finding Heidi and letting things happen, letting life decide.

He put on his yellow-and-black plaid jacket and flappy hat. The way to control the world, he thought, is to let things happen. That meant it was Heidi-time. Heidi was ripe, he could smell, he could almost taste the ripe rank melon of her juicy sex. Just thinking of those scenes woke the masses the fuck up. The galaxy stirred. The Skein dreamed. The Foam bubbled and frothed.

They got the message and so did he. This time it was clear. Sic her, Jack. Sic her!

He raced into the street and across the city, baying like a hound inside, a willing prize for the lucky woman who won him and didn't even know it yet.

But knew how to do improv, knew how to go with the flow, knew how to say yes.

www.ingramcontent.com/pod-product-compliance
Lightning Source LLC
Chambersburg PA
CBHW071238130626
46556CB00003B/1058